Malcolm's version:
'Brenda,' I said, 'yo⸺

'I know,' she said. 'I wrote it.'

I was patient. 'But why?'

'Well, if I hadn't you'd have wondered why McLofty gave you a blank piece of paper.'

Which confirmed once and for all that she was completely incapable of holding an intelligible conversation.

Brenda's version:
We sat down and I waited for him to observe the common courtesies but it seems he'd missed that afternoon at charm school.

A minute took two to tick by. Then: 'I got your note,' he said.

'I guessed.'

'How?'

'You're here.'

You don't get dialogue like that in *Neighbours*. Well, perhaps you do.

In alternate chapters Brenda and Malcolm tell of how they met and how their unlikely relationship somehow managed to stagger from one disaster to the next.

To Maeve

Watching

Jim Hitchmough

BANTAM BOOKS
TORONTO · NEW YORK · LONDON · SYDNEY · AUCKLAND

WATCHING

A BANTAM BOOK 0 553 11034 5

First publication in Great Britain

PRINTING HISTORY
Bantam Books edition published 1990

Novelisation copyright © Jim Hitchmough 1990

Watching copyright © Granada Television
Limited 1990

This book is set in 10/10½ Century Textbook
by Colset Private Limited, Singapore.

Bantam Books are published by Transworld Publishers
Ltd., 61–63 Uxbridge Road, Ealing, London W5 5SA, in
Australia by Transworld Publishers (Australia) Pty. Ltd.,
15–23 Helles Avenue, Moorebank, NSW 2170, and in
New Zealand by Transworld Publishers (N.Z.) Ltd., Cnr.
Moselle and Waipareira Avenues, Henderson, Auckland.

Reproduced, printed and bound in Great Britain by
BPCC Hazell Books Ltd
Member of BPCC Ltd
Aylesbury, Bucks, England

Chapter One

Life's just full of *ifs*, isn't it. *If* my Mum hadn't cut herself opening a tin of ravioli the night my Dad fell down the steps of the Rose of Mossley they'd never have met. Least it's most unlikely. Not in the Royal Infirmary Outpatients, I shouldn't think. They might have met somewhere else but I doubt it.

We are, as our Pamela so frequently points out, the product of a mixed marriage. She attributes lots of things to this; her weight problem, our Gerald being a bone idle illiterate (or dyslexic, as Mum calls it), me being a messer and always being in trouble and upsetting people just because I say what I think instead of thinking what I say and always rabbiting on and forgetting what I was talking about in the first place and not listening to the advice of people who are older and wiser like her, well certainly older and where was I?

Oh yes, the mixed marriage. Well, they do go on about these things round here. I mean, it wasn't as if they had different politics or different religions or one liked Persil and the other preferred margarine. No, it was just a matter of different breeding stock. His lot were Evertonians whereas hers wore red. Admittedly the hereditary difference stretched back as much as two generations but I couldn't believe it would have such far-reaching effects. Except to make our Gerald support Tranmere Rovers and me and Pamela dislike football altogether, which I suppose is much the same thing.

And *if* they hadn't met, then our Pamela wouldn't have happened at all, let alone been four months premature in which case I wouldn't have had an older sister to move in with when it was democratically decided (Voting three to one with one abstention) that I should leave home. Except of course that if they hadn't met then I wouldn't be around either. Least, I don't think so. For years they told everybody I was adopted and even I believed them until I was about thirteen. Then our Pamela took me to one side and explained in confidence that I wasn't adopted really. It was just that neither of them would accept the responsibility.

And *if* Pamela hadn't forgotten her flask that day I wouldn't have taken it to her, the history teacher wouldn't have fallen over the litter bin, and I wouldn't have been in The Grapes when Malcolm Stoneway called. Then just think how different life might have been. No one-wheeled bidet, no Cuthbert the Cupboard, no lesser-spotted gobtwit.

Least I don't think so. There is, of course, the Malcolm Stoneway theory that says these things would happen anyway. That the first *if* is only one starting trap and if you miss it you'll pop up in the one next door, or the one next door to that, the point being that when the gates open you still find yourself out on the same course, in the same Grand National with the same set of jumps that have already been mapped out for you in that great Filofax in the sky. I mean, it's so obviously Malcolm, isn't it? Who else could mix that many metaphors?

She's a big girl, our Pamela, and she needs to keep her strength up. That's why when I realised she'd left her one-litre flask of low cal. unsweetened decaffeinated soya soup with croutons sitting on the kitchen table I knew it was vital that I get it to her by lunchtime or she'd not have the strength to push the lift button when she left work that day. I was due a courtesy call at Mum's anyway; I mean, I'm not one to hold a grudge, and after all Nan had abstained – being out of the room at the time and, well, where was I? Oh yes, St John's Gardens. That's where Pamela

6

fed her face and indirectly most other parts when the weather was nice and her boss Mr Clough wasn't being. I was right. Well, I knew he wasn't being because she'd been home early every night that week.

Approaching from downwind I saw this goofy-looking nerd sitting next to her, far too close than was respectable and certainly not leaving enough bench for even a delicate little bot the size of mine to settle.

Inspiration comes easy at these times and so I took a card from my bag, went up to Pamela and asked in my best Crosby Hairdresser voice if she'd care to take part in a survey. You'd have thought it was a routine we'd worked before but honest to God it was straight off the cuff.

'It's on behalf of the Department of Health. Have you had any of these infectious diseases?' I asked, handing her the card.

Cool as anything she takes it and says, 'Let's see. Yes, yes, and that one. Yes, yes, and I've still got that one, and that one. In fact you could put me down for a full house.'

Well, Nerd is earwigging this and is already feeling the crawlies Tarzaning across from Pam's ample locks and straight down the back of his neck. So with a squirm, a wriggle and a wince he's up and away heading for home and a bath in neat Dettol. Before he'd gone ten yards he turned to see if Pamela or perhaps just a representative sample of her bugs, was chasing him, only to go A over T across a litter basket. Brilliant.

Amazing how the best ones aren't planned; just pure inspiration.

On the basis of his last trick I had him down as a failed acrobat but Pamela reckoned he was a history teacher. Dumb as he looked I couldn't see him as quite that bad.

I gave Pamela her flask which for the moment she wasn't desperate for, as she was still daintily disposing of a Tupperware box of sarnies made from two thick-sliced loaves and half a sheep. I commented in a sisterly

7

way on how well she was keeping to her diet which she accepted though admitting to being three weeks ahead.

Seeing as how the sisterly love was free flowing she then asked me how I'd got on the night before. She's nasty like that. You see, she knows I have amazingly bad luck with boyfriends. No matter how good a prospect they look to start with, they all turn out to be thick, or easily offendable, or naïve or all of these things put together. Then of course I can't be bothered with them.

Trouble is, I happen to have the most cynical and vindictive sister since Cinderella and she's always making out that it's them who give me the push.

Cow.

She reckons they bunk off because I take the mick out of them all the time but of course she's completely wrong. I mean, if they weren't so stupid I wouldn't have to make a dull evening a bit more entertaining by, well, saying things, and doing things. Just to stop everybody dozing off.

The particular Neanderthal she was on about was a big hairy lump from Widnes who I'd met at a disco the previous Saturday. He told me he'd got a summer job at Chester Zoo which I reckon was probably as a stand-in so the orangutan could go for his summer fortnight in Ibiza. You've probably seen him there. Of course Pamela didn't believe this but I told her that we would never have made a go of it, being completely incompatible. I don't believe in the yeti and he was one.

Before she could come back I switched to the attack and asked her about her boss. Cloughie is the deputy assistant undermanager brackets claims in the Bootle and Bournmouth Assurance Company, and he and our Pamela have an 'understanding'. I don't know what that means but I think it's naughty and I'm sure it's something Mrs Cloughie doesn't know about.

Pam has worked with the B. and B. since leaving school last century, and has been in his department for the last three years, so I think it's a case of familiarity breeds. Certainly she always goes dead defensive when I bring up the subject. Anyway, although I've never met him I know I'll manage to dislike him intensely when I do.

It seemed that for this particularly sunny lunch hour midst the waving daffodils and bombing pigeons he was far too busy to share a sandwich with her. Ah!

Then I saw him. A ripe and scrawny wino who was methodically inspecting the contents of all litter bins in the North-West of England. I waited until Pam had taken a large bite and then asked, 'Is this your Mr Clough coming now?'

Then I'm off with a, 'See you in The Grapes at six', knowing that any smart reply she might have is locked in tight behind a gob-full of sheep sandwich.

The atmosphere at Mum's was just a bit cool going on frigid. Our Sandra was there with this new fella of hers and I could tell Mum didn't like him. He was a biker. All black leathers and studs everywhere (well, so Sandra said). He was mouthing off about some Hell's Angels' rally he was going to that Sunday in Rhyl. Sandra was dead keen but Mum just bristled. She's a great bristler. Mum went on about how these things could turn nasty but I must admit it did seem pretty exciting. Some of the things they get up to. Wow! And on a motor bike! Problem was that, although he was acting the hard case, it didn't quite come off. I mean he had the boots, the earring, the dirty finger nails and even HAT tattooed on his knuckles. But somehow the great macho image was spoiled by him being about three-foot-six. He looked like a handbag with feet.

(Later I asked our Sandra why HAT and she said it was going to be HATE but the tattooist wouldn't do any more on account of her fella starting to cry.)

Mum's subtle way of letting Sandra know she didn't like him was to keep going to the front door to wonder what those kids were doing to that bike. Each time, the handbag ran out and counted the wheels or whatever until finally he got fed up. He gave out with a few grunts that meant he was leaving, whereupon Sandra slipped her front door key into her bra, grabbed her helmet and followed. Next Nan's away too, heading for her Over Sixties club. She said it was a talk entitled 'Arthritis: Need it affect your performance?' but we didn't believe her. So there was just me and Mum.

I've got to be frank. We've never really been like bessie mates, me and Mum. I got off to a bad start even before I was born, it seems. Too busy kicking her belly from the inside and forgetting to somersault in time for the big entrance. So I came breech. Typical she says. And that's the way it's always been. Me getting things the wrong way round; putting my foot in it; not using my head. Oh yes, she's dreamed up more significances from that little incident than Sigmund Freud at a Tell Us Your Dirty Dreams Party. What she forgets is that it wasn't my fault. I wasn't really in charge at the time. Nor since come to that. I don't mean to be a messer – to say these things, but I just get triggered and I see something and I say something. Straight from eyes to tongue without going through my brain. But I have got one. Even she admits that. Just that it's never been out of the polythene.

Since I left home though me and Mum have been running pretty smooth. Only seeing each other about once a week helps, of course. Also there's a sort of unspoken truce which works because I count ten every time she asks me a personal question and she doesn't ask any. Well, that's what we each mean to do and we almost succeed.

So when she waves the olive branch and suggests I stay for tea I usually do. Except for this time. And that's where some more of the big *ifs* come into things. *If* Pamela hadn't forgotten her flask I wouldn't have taken it to her and *if* I hadn't taken it to her I wouldn't have said I'd see her in The Grapes at six and *if* it hadn't been just past five when Mum asked me to stay

I could have rung Pam at the office to let her know but I couldn't so I didn't. Of course I explained all this to Mum who naturally preferred not to understand – so I left.

The Grapes is our watering hole. The beer is weak and the spirits watered but we don't mind. We only go in there for the company. Not that we ever speak to anyone. That would be against the rules. And nobody gets bevvied these days. Only scallies and wallies and kids on their way home from school. Of course if we ever do need a drink we can always rely on Harold. Harold is the regular barman there with a pair of specs like the bottoms of two Schweppes mixers. If you're thirsty you can always down it and then tell him it was the wrong pump. Given the amount of slops and water they feed back into the mild two for the price of one is probably about fair.

Then why do we go? Well, it's handy; just round the corner from the flat and the next nearest is The Wheatsheaf and one of us got banned from there for accidently fusing the jukebox – four times. I say one of us because it wasn't quite clear who he was screaming at when he told us to leave but Pam tagged along too. Actually she likes that sort of music but she was in a way equally responsible. I mean, I know I put it into the plug, but it was her fag packet that provided the silver paper.

Our patronage (I like that word) of The Grapes depended really on how well things were in a plastic kitchen on a plastic estate in a plastic place called Frodsham some twenty miles away. That's where Mrs Clough frequently chose to 'not understand' her plastic husband which resulted in him crying on my darling sister's ample buzzoom. No plastic there, believe me. Actually, I've never been to Frodsham and maybe it's a dead good place. I always see places as like the people who nest there – until I find out different – and the more I hear about Cloughie the yukkier Frodsham gets.

11

But there again Pamela likes him. So maybe her Frodsham is all thatched cottages and honeysuckle growing up the bus shelters. Either way there seemed to be a truce in operation in the plastic kitchen so for a time the buzzoom remained undented. And we were in The Grapes for a diluted vodka and chat.

Chat is really the wrong word. Me and Pam never chat, we spar. I don't know if other sisters are like this, or brothers come to that, but it's as if chatting is too easy. Chatting is what you do with somebody you don't know or don't like. Dead boring. So we take chat and knock it about, take meanings that aren't meant, and make sentences that aren't sense. It's great. Like turning a game of pat-a-cake into a karate work-out. And I like it, particularly because I always win. Yes, Pam may have a job, and money for clothes and her own flat – I'm only a guest – and a steady relationship, and be popular at work, but I've got a black belt in the old repartee.

Mind, she's not far behind; probably a brown belt. Whereas Malcolm, well, he better hang on to his trousers. But I'm jumping ahead.

I've always liked words. I could read before I went to school. Pam taught me. She was seven years older than me, about five now, and we had a special relationship. I could always go to her with my problems, and she'd laugh. At school they never taught me anything new. In fact I reckon the whole eleven years was a waste of time. I used to write crazy word essays when I was nine but they didn't like them much. They said you must never start a sentence with 'and' or 'but' and spelling was very important if you were to have any hope of getting a real job like a typist and although I didn't split my infinitives I'd broken everything else – so I stopped for ever.

Least I stopped writing for them. I carried on sending seventeen-page letters to my cousin in Canada in exchange for her annual postcard of Niagara Falls and I still write to the girl who used to live next door who moved to Bristol and there's my diary. I read a lot.

12

It's one of the privileges of unemployment. I've four library tickets in my name and four in Pamela's, which reminds me, I must tell her she owes three quid in fines.

That evening in The Grapes we decided on a bit of People Watching. It's our game. It started in my happy before-school days when big sister pushed me round Tesco's in a trolley with my laces tied through the grating to stop me climbing out. Of course Pamela was the older responsible sister who could do all the shopping, the ironing and vacuuming when she was eight months old – if you believe Mum. Me, being a prize messer, still can't cope with any of them at twenty – if you'd believe her again. Trouble is, she's right.

So I'm in the trolley. To keep me occupied Pam would get me to guess what the other shoppers were like. 'What about that old biddy in the green coat and headscarf?' (Probably be all of twenty-four.) And I'd think, and notice things. 'She's got a baby, a cat and has just been to the bingo.' 'OK, Sherlock, why?' 'She bought Rusks, Whiskas and she's got a pencil stub stuffed in her rollers.'

We played the game on buses, in picture queues, even in the pictures if the film was boring – and it always was. I've been shushed so much, that I miss it when I'm home on my own watching a video.

Then later at discos and pop concerts but using our own special sign language. I just loved our Pam's sign for a decrepit old poser. Of course the straight guessing got a bit boring even early on, so we used to elaborate a bit. Well, not so much a bit as a lot; and later entirely. The winner was the one whose description was the most way-out. This meant that we could do the regulars in the pub over again which is how I came to be assessing Cedric on the night in question, your honour.

Septic Cedric is a horrible dollop of greaseball who slimes his way into The Grapes most evenings leaving a silver thread across the floor and a mouthful less in

any pint that the owner turns his back on. I offered
my latest version of his origin suggesting that he was
the result of an early test tube baby experiment –
before they realised they should wash the test tubes
out first.

I then suggested that Pam might care to have a
crack at Mousey Mary, another regular who we'd not
done for a while, when the door opened and in he came.

CHAPTER TWO

If Mr Ambrose hadn't suddenly decided we ought to
restock the tie racks and if Terry had helped instead of
saying he had to leave early because he'd promised his
landlady he'd pick up a couple of plaice fillets from
Marks because she particularly likes them, I would
have got away on time. As it was, by the time I got to
Victoria Street the tunnel traffic was backed up to
North John Street. Well, almost; it certainly reached
that traffic island near the top, which is why I decided
it might be quicker to nip down Mathew Street and
then come out half-way along Whitechapel except
that there was a van unloading near the top and I
couldn't get through. It was then that I decided that
as I was going to be late, I might as well be even later
so after negotiating a rather difficult U-turn just outside Cavern Walks I headed south towards Aigburth.

As it happened, this wasn't the master stroke I'd
intended, as a lorry had broken down at the end of
Paradise Street, by the Moat Hotel, well the far side of
it actually, so that there was single-line traffic for at
least half a mile, possibly three-quarters, certainly
five-eighths. Eventually I decided to nip up towards
Sefton Park and to cut across that way. Then, would
you believe it, a burst water main.

So what with the delay at the shop and my mini-tour of central Liverpool and the water gushing down Ullet Road I realised I needed to stop somewhere for a 'you know what'. Amazingly, just as I reached this decision I turned a corner and there, low and behold, right in front of me was a pub. Unfortunately that was a bit too soon after reaching the decision so I drove on a bit until I eventually came to one called The Grapes.

Actually, I didn't notice the name at the time. It wasn't really significant.

I went in. I must admit to never being quite comfortable in this sort of situation. I even feel self-conscious walking into a pub back home in Meols. I just wish you could sort of materialise in the middle of a group, already holding a glass and talking nonchalantly, instead of having to trek across from door to bar watched out the corner of the eye by everybody there. Though I suppose materialising would tend to attract attention too. You can't win.

My first mistake was to turn right and go through a door at the end which simply led to another bar. Then I couldn't get back because someone was leaning on the door and I had to go out into the road, along the pavement and back in, the way I had originally. I mean, it sounds easy but coming in that second time took a hell of a lot of courage. My instinct was just to get back on the bike and find another pub but more basic pressures prevailed, if you see what I mean.

So with my helmet held firmly under my arm I crossed to the bar and asked a bloke leaning there where the Gents was. With an unnecessarily expansive gesture he indicated a corridor at the far end. As I reached the door, wasn't it just my luck to meet a stock Scouse comic on his way out who pointed at my helmet and said, 'No need to bring your own mate. They've got big ones in there.'

The thing about Scousers is not so much that they are particularly funny but they are quick. Given any situation there's a smart remark spat out before normal human beings have time to focus. I can take them in small doses. *Very* small doses. It's not that

15

the rest of us don't think of some devastating riposte too. It's just that it's well past its 'sell by' date when we do.

I'm a bit of an expert on this subject actually as I've studied the tribe at close quarters for most of my life. I was born in Slough which is about twenty miles due west of London but my folks, who were originally from the North, moved back to Chorley when I was two. Well, twenty-two months actually. Chorley is in Lancashire, about twenty miles north-west of Manchester, or twenty miles north-east of Liverpool, whichever you prefer.

Dad was with the DHSS and when I was nine he was promoted to the main Liverpool office so we moved to the Wirral. Meols actually, right on the sea front. He died three years later.

A heart attack. Just the one; no mild coronary to warn him to take things easy. No amber flashing light. Slow down you're doing too much. No, just one; massive they called it. Devastating, it was. Not having him around, puffing on his pipe, frowning at his crossword or sorting through his picture postcard collection left a terrible blank. He was a warm and generous man and I can picture him like that even now, though it's not quite accurate because he didn't smoke. But he did collect postcards. All neatly filed, labelled and cross referenced.

The oddest thing was that in one way nothing changed. Mum had always run the house, the finances, me, him. So things carried on much as was on a day-to-day, business-as-usual, routine, outward appearances basis. But I missed him. A lot. Mostly it was his approval I missed. He admired everything I did, was interested in all my interests and helped just enough to defuse a frustration yet leaving enough of a problem so that when you sorted it, you had the satisfaction of having really done it all yourself, to all intents.

My mother continues to run things very well considering, because I don't think the pension is all that much, but the house is paid for and although we don't run to a car I have the bike – which reminds me. I glanced outside to check that it was still there and then went back to the bar to order a half of bitter. I thought that by the time I'd drunk it the traffic might have eased and after all I had used their facilities and, well, you know how it is. Trouble was, I couldn't get near the bar, nor could I attract the attention of the barmaid. Of course, this is nothing new. I've always had this problem. I can be dead centre of a row of people at the bar of The George in Hoylake and Alice will serve everyone of them but me and then start on the ones who've moved in to replace them. It's as if I'm transparent.

Anyway, I had just given my third hopeful wave when it happened. This young Scots girl must have been standing close behind when, blow me, if I didn't knock her drink with my elbow. Embarrassment plus plus. But she didn't seem too upset, not like the drink (that's a joke), once I offered to replace it. So next I was waving for a half of bitter and a vodka and lime but still to no effect. Not, that is, until she borrows a penny, tosses it amongst the feet of the people in front of us and then says in a very posh voice: 'I say, is that a pound coin on the floor?'

Of course the whole crowd scrum down and I'm straight in with the order. I was impressed. The move was funny and effective and I wasn't at all surprised when she said she was from Glasgow. They're quick too.

She was nice. Easy to talk to, or rather to listen to; something of an aerobics expert and she was down here visiting her cousin, and helping with some new fitness programme he'd devised. She asked what I was doing Sunday and when I told her she laughed a lot. Lovely sense of humour, though she insisted on calling me Arnold. Before I knew it we had a date.

Tunnel entrance at ten.

CHAPTER THREE

For once in my life I was early. Didn't mean to be but sometimes everything just conspires to go right in spite of your best efforts. Of course the fact that Pamela was snoring away like a tug boat in the fog, having been busy with overtime activities extending way beyond the call of stenographing, had something to do with it. So I could have a bath and not get moaned at for taking all the hot water, borrow her make-up without being screamed at and try on three of her tops and a jumper without fear of decapitation. Mind, I finished up wearing my own gear. I mean, I know baggy was in that year but me in Pamela's togs is just tentsville. I'm beginning to wonder if she doesn't keep her Giant Haystacks physique just to avoid being democratic in the wardrobe department. She's that tight.

So there I was in the car park by the tunnel entrance, and didn't my gorgeous biker cruise up on a machine so black, so powerful, so throaty that my toe nails cut through my shoes. He didn't see me right away so I tip-toed up behind him and gave an 'anybody home' tap on his helmet. A big helmet it was. One that could hide a face completely, and that's just what I needed when he took it off. I felt myself scarleting so hot my eyelash glue was melting. He grinned. I dried. And then putter puttering into the car park came the real Arnold.

If I hadn't been so embarrassed about knocking on this other fellow's helmet I'd have walked out there and then. But you don't, do you. They talk about wanting the ground to open and swallow you – well, it's true. And for me, the hole in the ground was the sidecar tacked onto Arnold's bike. Otherwise there's no way I'd ever have climbed into that thing in the first place. Crazy, isn't it. I made a mistake and felt I must look a right wally in the eyes of some stranger, so I dive into the first escape tunnel that comes along and finish up looking a mega wally in the eyes of the whole world and Birkenhead. But it happened. Another of the big *ifs*, you see. *If* Pamela hadn't had a late night she'd have been awake in time to moan at me and make me late, and I'd have arrived after Arnold, seen from a safe distance him and his antique sewing machine with the semi-detached goldfish bowl, and done a runner.

So it's all her fault really.

The trip through the tunnel was bad. We got stuck behind a lorry that belched diesel fumes like dry ice at a pop concert and twice as smelly. The sidecar had been carefully constructed so as to produce a steady draught up through the floor so it slowly filled with fumes. I pulled the canvas top back to let them out but this just let more in, so I settled to writing my will on the steamed-up windscreen. There was worse to come. At least the tunnel road surface was smooth. When we hit the original Druids' road through deepest Wirral I got bounced around so much three fillings shot out.

I suppose it must have been a punishment. My Mum was dead against our Sandra going to any Hell's Angels' Rally and I'd sort of agreed with her. Then the same day didn't I chat up this biker in The Grapes and get him to take me with him for a fun day Sunday, knowing it would be next stop Rhyl with a ton or two of ton-ups. He didn't actually say where he'd be going but they play it very close to their leathers these bikers; least the real cool ones do. Not like the handbag.

So that was it. My punishment for being a hypocrite, but you can only take so much. After half an hour that seemed like half a week I put my hand through the lid and waved a hanky. Perhaps I could get time off for bad behaviour. The response was a lot later than immediate. First I got a grin and a wave that reminded me why I'd christened him Arnold in the first place. He looked like one. But finally he got

19

the message and we stopped at a country caff in the middle of nowhere. You couldn't imagine the relief. It had been like riding in a liquidiser. I told him, 'A couple more miles of that and you'd have had a sidecar slopping with puréed Brenda.'

He gave me a very strange look.

CHAPTER FOUR

Leonard had rung on Thursday evening. He had seen a hen harrier out on Burton Marsh and told me the precise spot. I wasn't too hopeful. This had happened before. You see, a lot depended on the tides, and the week before there had been a high spring at Parkgate. Trouble was, I could never remember whether you got the time of high water by adding an hour every day or taking one off. As things turned out my calculations were quite academic. Having first agreed to pick up the Scots girl by the tunnel entrance (Liverpool end) early Sunday morning it then turned out that the soonest she could make it was 10 am. It was unfortunate but understandable. The problem was that before she left the house she had to see to her invalid sister.

This meant that we wouldn't arrive on the Marsh until about eleven, maybe even quarter past, by which time normally I'd be well into my second flask of decaffeinated. She obviously hadn't been birdwatching before as she was dressed in a sort of day-glow orange that would make her visible from the other side of the Dee estuary, but there was no point in saying anything. When you introduce somebody to a new activity you've got to go a bit at a time and you've got to be positive. Never dampen enthusiasm. Especially a girl's. That's what Terry says. He's the chap I work with and I must admit I'm interpreting his maxim more broadly than his randy self would intend, but I'm sure it still applies.

The first shock came when I pulled in at a café. I think she had the same problem as had afflicted me on the occasion of our first meeting and she waved for a stop. We hadn't spoken when I'd picked her up at the tunnel entrance, as she seemed to be in a bit of a hurry for us to get away. I didn't even cut the engine. Then, as I helped her out of the sidecar, she let rip with a nasal winge of pure Scouse that I found depressingly familiar. Having lived in the area for so long now I hardly notice it, but when you do meet someone from abroad, Glasgow in this case, you do look forward to a little *badinage* in a different register.

'Hold on a minute,' I said. 'Where do you come from?'

She gave me a funny look.

'Are you soft or somethin'? I just got out the bloody sidecar.'

Which just about set the tone for the day. It had all been a big act. She wasn't helping with any training, she knew nothing of aerobics, and she wasn't even the most distant relative of Kenny Dalglish.

You may find it hard to credit that I could have believed any part of her meanderings in the first place. I do myself. But, you see, she is expert, and in the ensuing months I witnessed her fool more cynical types than me. Terry Milton for one and it took a bewhiskered French Canadian with a wooden leg to settle that score.

But I did believe and that's my problem. Even after twenty years in this land of the fairy tale I still can't get out of the habit of believing people. Silly, isn't it? Actually thinking that when someone strings together a sequence of words that there should be sense to the sentence, sincerity in the syntax, instead of fabrication, fantasy and falsehood. (I can be quite poetic when roused.) Particularly when it's a perky lass with a pretty face and a smile that can light a room. Now that I've known her longer I can see that I must have been easy pickings – but I'm sure that accent would have fooled Billy Connolly himself. And the smile, devastating, but it's seldom in use. Most of the time she's on continuous moan with auto reverse.

So she carped, about the bike, about the sidecar, about the smell. She asked what I kept in it speculating that it might be dead gerbils. She relished the word as well as the image and I knew I'd copped a regular scally with 'O' level mockery, a sharp tongue and the regulation-issue razor wit that comes with the Scouse uniform. Well, I'd just have to make the best of it. After all she was keen to come and it's a lot more fun with two, as Terry would say.

I know the café well; it's sort of mid-Wirral, perhaps a bit nearer the Dee than the Mersey though not much and nicely placed as a staging post. That's about the only thing nice about it. The proprietor is a miserable old grouse who makes out he's doing everyone a favour even being there. Serving coffee then becomes a gesture of such magnanimity that you feel you should send him a thank-you card. My ultimate impertinence in asking for biscuits left him speechless. Sadly the condition was not infectious and Brenda continued to whine. I say Brenda but at that point I was wondering if the name was just as false as the potted life history she'd given me over her replacement vodka and lime. These doubts were enhanced when she insisted on calling me Arnold though I'd told her my name was Malcolm, a mistake she justified by telling me I looked like an Arnold.

'And what does an Arnold look like?' I asked, whereupon she emphatically established the intellectual level of the conversation by replying.

'You, you daft bugger.'

At one point the quiet of the café was disturbed by some greasy-looking bikers at a corner table who started arm wrestling and mouthing and generally fouling the image of the motor cycle fraternity. This prompted a very strange enquiry from Brenda:

'Do you think they're going where we're going?'

I replied that they didn't look the type, and got an enigmatic, 'Nor do you.' She then asked how I got to know about meetings and I explained about the club and our monthly magazine. When I mentioned that my friend Leonard was chairman this year she was obviously impressed, although she seemed a little confused in the matter of terminology as she then asked:

'Of the chapter?'

It seemed an appropriate time to move on.

CHAPTER FIVE

I told him straight that there was no way I would travel one more lousy inch in that stupid goldfish bowl. There was a vacant length of saddle sticking out behind him which I was quite prepared to keep warm.

'I'll get on the back and hang on to you,' I explained.

'But you can't,' he pouted. 'It's not allowed. Not without a helmet.'

Would you believe it? All the bikers in the world and I had to pick one who'd got an *I Spy* badge for law. Well, given all the clues I'd had up to that point I should have guessed there was something phoney about the whole gig. But I was tired. I'd had a bad week, and what with a cold and sitting through *Krypton Factor*, *Mastermind*, two rounds of *University Challenge* and three *Blockbusters* my brain was sore. So it was back in the sidecar, but not for so long this time. I only lost one filling, caught my earring on the back of the seat, laddered my tights on something sharp sticking out of a canvas bag at the front end and broke my right thigh with my chin when we stopped suddenly. A doddle really. So I was just wondering if I should write my address in blood on the canvas bag so that they'd have somewhere to send the bits, when the lid opened. I peeped out and round. We were in Central Nowhere.

'What's up?' I asked.

'We're here,' he jested.

'Here?' I puzzled. 'Where the bloody hell's here?'

'Burton Marsh,' he lied, for the bike was not slowly sinking.

This was the first sign he'd given of having a sense of humour, so I sat back and waited for the punch line. But there wasn't one. Or rather that was it. He was, would you believe, a birdwatcher. We'd gone all that way to look at bleeding sparrows!

What can you do? He offered to run me into Neston and put me on the next bus to civilisation, or Birkenhead. It was cold, there was rain in the air and we were surrounded by a billion acres of green nothing but I thought, what the hell, I'll stick around for a bit. When it comes to stupid, I've got badges.

Of course, once I took my brain out of neutral it was all so obvious. Him a biker! Even his leathers looked like off-cuts from a worn settee. No studs, no earrings, no wrist chains, nothing manly at all. And what I'd taken to be the edge of a tattoo peeping out from under his cuff turned out to be a biroed phone number.

We left the bike rusting under a tree and set out on a hike across a field that was probably Cornwall. This gave me time to think and time to worry. The thing that bothered me was the possibility that our Pam might find out. If she ever discovered that my little chat-up had got me no further than a Wirral Marsh with a poncy birdwatcher, after me saying I was heading for a Rhyl rave-up, she'd laugh till her shoes were full. So I asked him just one favour:

'Promise you won't tell our Pamela.'

'I wouldn't know your Pamela if I fell over her,' he sniffed.

'Some fall,' I pictured. 'You'd break your neck. She's thirteen stone and twelve of them's her bum.'

24

(You don't get repartee like that in Manchester.) 'She was sitting in the corner by the space invaders.'

He stopped and if there'd been a glass plate in his head you'd have seen the cogs turning.

'I didn't notice her.' Wait for it. 'Or her friends!'

It was the first of what I've come to recognise as a 'Malcolm joke'. Not completely unfunny, interesting because of its rarity value and carefully heralded by a smile that lifted like a pair of stage curtains as he first thought of it himself, then delivered with the finesse of a lumberjack.

We now have an understanding. I've promised not to call him Arnold, and he's promised not to crack more than two jokes each month, except for December when he just cracks one – as a sort of Christmas bonus to the rest of us.

CHAPTER SIX

Brenda continued to bleat her way across the field as we headed for the line of bushes that edge the Marsh. The Scouse skewers were thrown with dull monotony until I finally returned a subtle barb that left her quite speechless. Can't remember it now but I could see she was both surprised and impressed. Something about Space Invaders. It prompted her to tell the truth about events leading up to our first encounter in The Grapes – and it was then my turn to be what she would call 'gob-smacked'.

The deviousness of the woman had no bounds. She confessed that, far from me knocking her drink over, she had come up behind me and pushed it against my elbow. What's more, although she had claimed it was a vodka and lime it was, in fact, a bitter lemon. It seemed the whole charade had been engineered in

25

order to get a lift to some Hell's Angels' Rally in Rhyl that Sunday. I could hardly credit the gall, the deceit, the duplicity.

Some might speculate that a higher power was equally shocked, and decided that her behaviour merited suitable retribution. They might also say that it was simply my misfortune to be chosen as the instrument, but not me. I wouldn't say that. I know it was already decided.

You see, I'm a determinist: a believer in predestination. What will happen, will happen. And it's true. Just you think back. Everything that was ever going to happen did actually happen. You can't argue with it. Just try and think of one incident that was going to happen that didn't; see, you can't.

This isn't to say I don't believe in free will. There is of course an element of choice in many of our minor activities, but such choices have no long term value. They are always balanced out, and our disappointments and frustrations are, in fact, the consequences of past peccadilloes or even future mischiefs as yet undreamed.

However, I must admit my faith has taken something of a battering since I met Brenda. I don't know if time will ever reach sufficient fullness for me to know why she has been visited upon me. But I'm sure there's some reason. Maybe she is a sort of punishment.

There was, of course, that incident many years ago when the Mersey Tunnel toll collectors were on strike, and honesty boxes were placed at each end. I hadn't got change so I just tossed in ten pence. But really – Brenda, as a punishment for that – well, it does seem a bit extreme.

Mind, it's not all been bad. Looking back from this distance there have been moments. Quiet moments, even occasionally tender moments. Moments when eyes met, fingers touched, a half smile semaphored a tender thought. But not many. No, not many moments like that. And when they did happen they usually

26

heralded some major catastrophe which set the relationship back so far you couldn't believe it would ever start up again. Like Batman and the Bikers, or the Bridal Car and the Bike Museum. B is very much her letter. B for Brenda and B for Balls-Up. Sorry. I'm rushing ahead. Back to Burton Marsh.

This was perhaps our first Moment. A very small moment but a Moment none the less. Brenda did little to hide her boredom with the whole ornithological experience and my attempts to hush her long enough for my hen harrier to show, were ever doomed to failure. She has that sort of nervous energy you see in some small kids, and you know that any promise you may extract to be quiet, be still, behave, has a shelf life of at most two minutes.

As I watched, she informed me that she was a watcher too. She and her sister had developed this rather tortuous game in which they guess the background of people from their appearance, manner, dress. All very Miss Marple and rather limiting, I thought. I've discovered since that the sport has developed somewhat surreal overtones and that assessments now rely more on absurd fantasy than genuine deduction. It fits.

I asked her about her own background and was not surprised to hear she was unemployed. I do not think this was so much a consequence of the general sickness but more to do with her. Brenda would have been unemployed in the sixties when there were jobs to spare (so the story goes.) Her anarchic manner and ill-considered and insulting prattle, complete with her indifference to any authority would turn off any possible employer. You can tell there's an intelligent life form in there somewhere – probably very intelligent – but it has obviously been so spoiled and misdirected in its formative period that it's no use to anyone. What a waste.

'Do you come here every week?' she asked. I told her most weeks, though there were other places.

'This is my favourite,' I explained. 'There's the

27

Marsh down there and that copse over to the right, well, all sorts nest in there.'

Immediately she curled her lip and said with crude inference, 'Do they now!' thus putting an end to any prospect of civilised conversation. I returned to my watching only to be subject to a mock stripper routine as she played for attention like a precocious four-year-old. She rendered a throaty version of the tune as she first shed a scarf then dropped a glove across my binoculars. I must admit I found the whole situation a little disturbing. I mean, I haven't exactly led a sheltered life but things were progressing in a manner that could well have got out of hand. I needed time.

'Please hush, Brenda,' I said, 'there's something moving in the rushes.'

'Probably Moses,' she replied.

Later she feigned sleep and when I asked her to pass a book from my jacket pocket I was subjected to the whole SAS bit with her crawling on her belly.

'Who dares wins, 'ey Malcy?' she said.

Malcy. She was the first and only person to call me that. I hate it. In desperation I decided it was best to ignore her and do what I had come to do.

At one point I thought I saw a sparrowhawk down near the copse. Mistakenly I thought aloud which prompted her to say, 'They'll do him for loitering.'

A play on the word 'copse', you see.

So it went on. I changed tack and tried to interest her. I offered her the binoculars but soon realised she hadn't really got the faintest idea.

'What happens?' she asked. 'When we see one don't we tick it off in your little book or something?'

I explained that it wasn't like train-spotting.

'They don't all have numbers on their side,' I joked. 'Hey, look. Here comes the 253 Inter City High Speed Snow Goose direct from Reykjavik.'

Of course, like so many who boast a great sense of humour, she couldn't take it when the joke was on her, so off she trounced back towards the bike in high dudgeon.

28

So that was it. A wasted day. Even the weather turned lousy and by the time we reached Liverpool it was bucketing down.

Why I ever took the trouble to return her earring I'll never know.

CHAPTER SEVEN

I couldn't believe it. How could a grown man go to a miserable dump like that week after week, crawling through soggy brambles in the hope of seeing some washed-out canary? I mean, if you're interested in that sort of thing you can see them dead close any time you care to switch on BBC 2. Then there was all the gear he took. Binoculars, wellies, a green hair net, and best of all this tripod thing he'd made to hold his binoculars steady. Very proud of it he was and he insisted on posing to show how it worked.

'Of course,' he said, 'I wouldn't be bending down like this.'

Which seemed very wise if there were other horni-thologists about.

'I have a little canvas stool.'

I suggested he told his doctor.

Then the rain came.

Going there had been bad but coming back was indescribable; but I'll try. There were still the bumps, the draughts, the smell of dead gerbils, but now for bonus there were drips of water from above and squirts from beneath piercing every crevice I've got and drilling a few new ones.

He dropped me at the end of our road. We didn't speak. I couldn't. I just gave him a look that would have pierced his skull if he hadn't been wearing a helmet.

My cold had now become triple pneumonia but I decided on a bath before I booked into intensive care.

29

Slowly sensation returned to my extremities and I lay there dreaming up revenge tortures for the Meols Angel.

By seven o'clock I was back in The Grapes with our Pamela dead suspicious as to why, if Rhyl was as great as I'd just told her it was, I was back so early. She's got a nose for these things: sharp and pimply. I told her it was all pretty wild to start with but the weather had put a damper on things. She sniffed her suspicion so I said we had had to leave in a hurry when the law recognised my escort. She frowned and worried if Sandra was OK. I reassured, and said that anyone with their own walking handbag was excused aggro. Then she got all big-sisterly and warned me about hard-case bikers and not getting too involved.

'You want to watch it with them types,' she said. 'They can get dead nasty when they're roused.'

I thought of mouldy Malcolm with his wellies, his binoculars and his hair net. I had to smile. Unfortunately I thought the last bit out loud and she picked up on 'hair net'. I explained that it was Hell's Angels' slang for helmet.

I was keen to change the subject having had to change everything else already. 'Look, Pam,' I said, 'it was interesting, but I wouldn't want to bother again. Not really my scene.'

That was big mistake number one, for next the feminine intuition was dusted off and she cracked on that he'd given me the elbow.

'You really fancy him, don't you,' she said. 'I can tell.'

When it comes to feminine intuition my sister's all male. I told her straight. 'Look, Pamela, there is one thing I can give you a cast-iron guarantee about. There is not the remotest chance of me seeing that fella ever, not ever again.'

And I meant it. I tried to change the subject and suggested some People Watching but she said she had to go. I guessed that somebody's wife wasn't understanding him again.

'I wish I could do shorthand,' I mused as she got up to leave. 'What'll you be taking down tonight?'

Being a bit short of a sense of humour she landed me one with her shoulder bag and flounced off Cloughiewards.

I might have left too. But I now had a dead arm as well as a half-full glass so I decided another few minutes would not be amiss. In fact it was a miss. A big miss. Another of those *ifs* in fact. *If* I'd left at the same time as Pam – gone home to the flat for a Sunday night's telly, two aspirins and a litre of Ovaltine, I'd not have seen the earring. I was miles away, I suppose, musing on the horrors of mobile liquidisers, when I saw this earring swinging a foot or so from my nose. On the far side of the earring was the Meols Angel dangling it at arm's length like an apprentice hypnotist.

He just appeared. I looked around to see if someone had been rubbing an old tea pot. No one had. Just him standing there like one.

'Where did you come from?' I asked.

'I just got out the bloody sidecar,' he said, cogging my line.

There was a pause in which he didn't go away. Then he told me he thought the earring was very pretty. I offered to buy him a pair and asked him when his birthday was.

'Third of September,' he said, without having to look at his diary or anything.

I might have guessed. A bloody Virgo. Obviously I was not being unfriendly enough for the next thing he said was: 'Can I sit down?'

'Don't know,' I said. 'Have you tried?'

He tried. Alongside me. He found it quite easy. I wondered why he wasn't back in Meols sitting in his spin drier and he explained that after he dropped me he had gone on to see his mother in Aigburth. I wondered how many mothers he'd got but it turned out there was just the one. She was visiting an aunty and he had called to see if Mummy wanted a lift home.

'In your sidecar?' I asked.

'Yes.'

'But she didn't.'

'No.'

'As mothers go she strikes me as very intelligent.'

He told me she'd been in it before but declined on this occasion because of the weather. That was the last straw. Fancy *him* telling me that the sidecar is not a good place to be in wet weather. Me who had been bumped and bruised and battered, shaken and squirted and soaked.

Two hours on a one-wheel bidet.

So I told him. And he left.

And I was really glad.

CHAPTER EIGHT

I was glad it was all over. I now had a fresh week ahead of me to forget all about that soggy Sunday. And her; especially her.

Trouble was, fresh weeks begin with Mondays (in *my* diary anyway) and Monday is a lousy day to start anything with.

Because I was running late my mother delivered my Bran Flakes to the bathroom – she often does, though I'll never know why. After all, you can't eat them in the shower – or if you try it will take you ages to finish. Then as I stepped out, the inevitable happened. Odd, isn't it, that if you close your eyes and drop a random piece of soap onto a lino-tiled bathroom floor the soap will always fall towards the one square of lino tile that is occupied by a dish of Bran Flakes. Try it.

I came downstairs and sat down to my poached egg on (brown) toast to find her googling over our new kitten.

'Say good morning to Beethoven,' she simpered.

'Morning, Beethoven,' I obliged.

'Don't talk with your mouth full, Malcólm,' she said. Typical.

Then I remembered it was the day my RSPB magazine was due; excitement plus plus. My pal Leonard had submitted an article on local wildlife, along with a picture I had taken, and he'd been told it would be in this month's issue. My mother leafed through the mag, ('Don't want you reading at the table, bleat bleat.') and there was my picture with the bold caption, 'An early Goose on the Dee'. I felt quite proud. It was, in fact, a lesser white-fronted but my mother could only comment that it looked pretty mucky to her.

I suppose it was seeing Leonard's name in print that jogged her memory.

'He rang yesterday,' she said. 'His car is in for service and he wondered if you would give him a lift to the club this evening. I said you would.'

It was true that I would. Was happy to, even. Just that you like to make decisions yourself, don't you; especially when you're thirty. So maybe it was because of that niggle of resentment, or maybe it was because I hadn't actually spoken to him myself, or maybe it was that cocktail of Mondays, Warings and Brenda (that's got to be favourite), but anyway, although I nodded assent I then managed to completely forget the arrangement – until almost too late.

I was late. Not a lot, just ten minutes; well, perhaps thirteen if you consider work to start when you actually set foot on the sales floor as opposed to when you enter the back door of the premises, but I have to take off my leathers and put them and my helmet in my locker and this can take anything from two to five minutes depending on the weather and the time of year (winter longer).

I'm not often late. In fact, very rarely am I late, but to hear Ambrose talk you'd think I was never in on time. He's from Edinburgh and he pipes on and on in this monotonous high-pitched voice making the same point over and over again. I don't understand it. Why do people have to be so pedantic?

Terry's not at all that way. No, his conversation is sort of clipped, incisive, gets to what he's got to say with a strict economy of words as if he'd rationed himself to so many for the day and he was conserving them.

He's from Hemel Hempstead.

So, once I'd survived half a morning of intermittent Scots sarcasm I was relieved when business slackened to a steady nothing and Ambrose went for his break. Terry was adjusting the window display and he called across: 'How d'you make out yesterday?'

On Friday I had told him about the incident in the pub the night before. I found myself wishing I hadn't. I played for time.

'What?' I said.

'The wee haggis. You were taking her on safari to deepest Wirral. Was she game?'

Typical Terry. If a man takes a girl anywhere, any time, any how, there can only be one reason. I wonder if they're all like that in Hemel Hempstead.

I gave an abridged account of the day's events and his eyebrows rose steadily as I explained the misunderstanding regarding her nationality, my activity, and our destination. As I spoke I realised even more just how big a mistake the whole day had been. I stopped as his eyebrows joined his hairline and I waited for the comments.

You see, Terry has been around. He was two years at our Reading branch and before that was at Croydon, so he's very worldly.

He joined us as assistant manager when Pop Watson retired last July. (Nice old stick, Pop Watson; played the organ at the United Reform over in Wallasey.) My mother was most upset. Not with Pop Watson. No, with Terry being appointed Number Two.

'Should have been you,' she said.

She was all for having a word with 'that man Ambrose' and I had a terrible job explaining that these decisions are made at a higher level. Higher, even, than Mr Ambrose. My early years at Warings had not actually been a blaze of glory. There had been that incident with the morning suit, the carnation and the steam press. Then there was the hair piece I put on the window dummy which belonged to the doctor from Southport. Both of those were Monday incidents as I recall.

Terry seemed to regard Brenda as a 'good bet'. For what I didn't ask. He then proceeded to instruct me on matters which, in an earlier age, would have been called wooing but today would, according to Terry's philosophy, rhyme with it but begin with *SC*. Get it? Sorry.

He went on in this vein for some time, sprinkling his discourse with snide comments about my ornithological tendencies.

'Remember at school they told you about the birds and the bees? Well, your problem is that you've concentrated entirely on the first and forgotten the other.'

'The other?' I queried.

'Exactly,' he smirked. 'I shall have to take you under my wing.'

'No need to get into a flap,' I rejoined. He wasn't expecting that. I don't often come back with a smart answer but when I do the effect is often quite devastating.

As Terry stood there devastated, Mr Ambrose arrived and piped that as the number of people interested in purchasing suits, ties, shirts or any other items of male vestment continued to hover at the zero mark I might as well take an early lunch. He can be very flowery.

CHAPTER NINE

You could say it was coincidence me being just across
the road when he went for his lunch. I mean, I might
have been cutting through to Mod Shops where the
previous week I'd seen this yellow top for £8.95,
except that it wouldn't really go with my navy skirt,
but on the other hand it might be all right with
Pamela's grey which I'd borrowed when she was three
stone younger and she'd probably forgotten by now
that it was ever hers anyway. You could say it; but
you'd be lying.

I'd seen the name 'Waring's' on the plasi-bags in his
sidecar when I'd been looking for things to stop the
leaks with and – oh don't remind me.

So I waited until he'd turned the corner and then I
went in. There was a blond fellow posing in the window
with the dummies; I gave him 3.4 for interpretation
but he didn't see me. Then a tall bloke came across and
said, 'Yes?' as if the last thing they ever wanted to see
in that place was a customer. I might have given him
the run around but didn't. Instead I just put on the
poshest voice this side of Lytham St Annes and asked
if I could speak to Mr Malcolm Stoneway. He said
he'd gone to lunch but would be back shortly; surprise,
surprise.

Well, I couldn't wait as I'd, 'left Mumsy stuck on a
double yellow'.

'May I leave a note?' I fluttered.

'Please do,' he fawned.

'Grapes. Six,' I pencilled and folded.

If McLofty peeped he'd have thought it was a green-
grocery order from a very tight hospital visitor.

You're probably wondering why. I mean, after all I
said about Malcolm and his boneshaker and that
miserable Sunday.

Well, it was another of those *ifs*, wasn't it? I suppose it's the same the world over. *If* two people are in a
room and one is warm and snuggly in bed and the

other is frenzied, frantic and late for work, no matter how late frenzied frantic is, she'll still find time to bitch at warm and snuggly, and tell her to do something. With Pamela it's always, 'and take that lot to the launderette.' Now, *if* she hadn't said that, then I wouldn't have noticed she was eating cold fish fingers for breakfast. Then I wouldn't have told her she was disgusting, and she wouldn't have started getting on at me about Sunday. OK, so I did describe him as a cross between Boris Becker, George Michael and Rambo. But I hadn't said which bits from each.

'Gave you the heave, didn't he?' she cackled. 'One afternoon with Babbling Brenda was enough for him, I suppose.'

Any sensible person would just have covered her head with the sheet and gone back to sleep, but not me. I have to come back with the subtle rejoinder. 'Watch it, Cod's 'ead,' I said. 'Fact is, he pleaded with me for another date, but I told him no dice.'

Always ready for a little gentle banter she snipes back with: 'Lyin' cow. I thought it was funny you being back so soon. He gave you the elbow, didn't he?'

So what else could I do?

I arrived at The Grapes and went in the side door to find him standing on tip-toe looking out of the front window.

'Relax,' I said, 'I'm here.'

But he claimed he wasn't looking excitedly out of the window to get first sight of my arrival. No, he was keeping an eye on the kid who was keeping an eye on his bike. Perhaps I should have left then.

We sat down and I waited for him to observe the common courtesies but it seems he'd missed that afternoon at charm school.

A minute took two to tick by. Then: 'I got your note,' he said.

'I guessed.'

'How?'

'You're here.'

37

You don't get dialogue like that in *Neighbours*.
Well, perhaps you do.

'Malcolm,' I explained, 'this is a pub. They sell, "drinks".'

He was a bit startled by this news, but in the end came to terms with it and I was finally settled behind a vodka and lime.

Pamela had a lot to answer for.

I asked him about the gents' outfitters he worked in and he described it and the two blokes I'd seen there in more detail than I really wanted. He said that the blond one was called Terry and was a very good dresser, so I told him about my Uncle from Huyton who thought he was a sideboard.

'He's a *window* dresser,' he said. 'Did you speak to him?'

'No point,' I explained. 'My aunty kept the table mats in his mouth. Views of the Lake District they were.'

We crossed purposes for another ten minutes or so before he lapsed into muse. Then: 'Brenda,' he said, 'why, if you saw me going for my lunch, did you leave the note? Why didn't you come across?'

'And I thought you were slow.'

'You know what I mean.'

'I couldn't,' I explained. 'I wasn't speaking to you.'

The logic of this perfectly reasonable statement seemed beyond him. Aren't fellas thick? Any girl would understand.

So I explained it gently to him. How, even though he had deceived me, pretending to be a biker when he was really just a prat, out of the goodness of my heart I was prepared to forget all that and give him another chance. Well, you'd think after a magni-brill gesture like that he'd be dead grateful but he switches straight into forward huff and says, 'What!?'

'Another chance,' I said.

'Look,' he puffed, 'I don't have to stand for this.' Which was really a non-problem as he was sitting down.

38

I decided it was time to back off a bit as now there was steam coming out of his ears and Pamela hadn't even appeared and the whole point was to show her that I could have him if I wanted and well, you know. Least it was most of the whole point.

So I introduced him to the delights of People Watching; it was pretty painful.

'See that heap of lard on the bar stool?' I said. 'That's Septic Cedric. Tell me about him.'

'In a brown suit?' says Malcolm.

'Wear what you like,' I told him. But he meant Cedric.

Malcolm suggested that he might be an office worker.

I told him to use his imagination and illustrated: 'He's a travelling salesman who flogs cat litter, budgie bells and tortoise varnish.'

Whereupon Malcolm immediately confirmed that he'd missed the whole point of the game by looking pleased and saying that he needed some cat litter.

'He doesn't have it with him, you bonehead,' I gently explained. 'That's his belly hanging out.'

He still didn't understand so I spelt it out: 'Look, Malcolm, I don't know he sells cat litter. I'm surmising.'

'Oh I see,' he lied. 'It's just that we've got a new kitten. It's called Beethoven.'

I counted to ten which wasn't nearly enough and then asked: 'Malcolm, are you playing this game? Now stop and think. How old?'

'Just eight weeks,' he said.

'Cedric!' I yelled.

'Shush, he'll hear you,' he panicked.

Weakly I explained that Cedric didn't know his name was Cedric, and I might have given in there and then if Pamela hadn't turned up.

Another big *if*, you notice. Yes, she's a *very* big *if*.

And another case of inspiration producing something far better than anything you could have planned.

39

'Tell you what,' I said, 'you try the one who's just come in.' Pam had stopped to speak to someone by the door.

It seems the principles of People Watching were just beginning to percolate for he did have a go, did Malcolm.

'Big, isn't she?' he said.

'Disgustingly,' I happily agreed.

He thought she looked vaguely familiar but I hurried him on before he thought any harder. He guessed that she was about twenty-six which was very generous even if it was correct. Then he hit his stride surmising that she was a lady wrestler; I liked it.

'Wrestles in mud,' he speculated, 'under the name Barbarous Barbara.'

Then with a giggle of enjoyment like the little boy who's just found there's more to do than just widdle with it, he expanded and soon she'd become Barbarous Barbara the Bootle Bouncer. And on: 'Her father plays left prop forward for Widnes.'

'And her mother right?' I offered.

He was laughing into his next guess when Barbara bounced across towards us. Slowly his face changed colour as her shadow fell across our table (plus two chairs, a bench and the space invader machine).

'So what's going on here?' she baritoned.

'Nothing,' he sopranoed.

'Like he says,' I harmonised.

Pamela informed us that her ears had been burning so I suggested next time she fought she borrow Mum's scrum cap.

Malcolm's cogs had turned a rev or three and a print-out appeared.

'You two know each other,' he said.

'Oh sorry,' I said, 'you haven't been introduced. Malcolm, this is Barbara. Pamela, this is Rambo.'

And I left to get another round in.

CHAPTER TEN

I did not think it was funny. Meeting someone for the first time is always a bit awkward and to have that someone under the impression that you had been saying things about them, especially unflattering things, even if you had, and even if it was just a game, and a game that the person played herself from all accounts, well, it's just not on, is it?

I mean, Pamela is quite a well-made girl and you wouldn't want to upset her – not that I felt intimidated or anything. Just that I wouldn't want to upset anybody. Not like someone I could mention who delights in doing just that. So when she left Pam and me sitting there the atmosphere was most strained.

Then I had an idea; I decided I ought to go and check that the young boy who had offered to keep an eye on my bike was still there. Some might say there was an element of cowardice in this action but not so; after all, I did go back.

Brenda had returned with drinks. You'd think after the damage she'd done she'd have apologised, or at least let up a bit. But it seems to be almost a disease with her. She asked if the bike was all right and then explained to Pamela that it was a vintage model.

'It's even older than you,' she said, which prompted an exchange of insults between them that I was pleased to be out of.

Probably sensing this, Brenda said: 'Anyway, Pamela, I think your hair's great, and these days you see some really smart yard brushes.'

Pamela, of course, turned on me, and I denied even mentioning a yard brush, which was true but I could tell she didn't believe me. I wasn't sad when she left to see somebody called Clough.

I remarked how annoyed she'd been and Brenda said: 'Only with you. Don't worry, she doesn't hold a grudge. Just try and avoid meeting her when she's on her way home from the Stadium.'

For a moment I was dubious.

'She doesn't really wrestle, does she?' I asked.

'Only with Mr Clough,' Brenda said, 'and she always loses.'

And so it went on. Inanities and insanities. I'd had enough. Being in Brenda's company could never be described as pleasant and I wondered why, given my experience of Sunday, I ever left myself open to another assault. I decided to leave, but back of my mind there was just one little niggle.

'Brenda,' I said, 'your note. It said, "Grapes. Six."?'

'I know,' she said. 'I wrote it.'

I was patient: 'But why?'

'Well, if I hadn't you'd have wondered why McLofty gave you a blank piece of paper.'

Which confirmed once and for all that she was completely incapable of holding an intelligible conversation. I decided to go. Again. But just one other thought: 'You said you sent the note because you weren't speaking.'

'Right .'

'But what did you mean by, "another chance"?'

'What do you think?' she said.

'Did you mean a day out?'

'If you like, but not birdwatching. I'd as soon stay home and watch underwater darts from Barnsley.'

I took a deep breath. I don't know how but somehow I found myself arranging another outing, when really it was the last thing on earth I wanted. She twists things, you see.

Then I heard myself say, 'Perhaps Buxton or somewhere?'

'Given the choice,' she said, 'I think I'd prefer somewhere.'

And instead of leaving I found myself ordering her another vodka and lime and me a non-alcoholic lager.

I quite like it actually.

Then I glanced at my watch.

CHAPTER ELEVEN

'Oh hell,' he said.

I warned him about swearing in The Grapes. Harold may be blind but he's not deaf.

But it got worse.

'Casserole,' he said.

My delicate sensibilities were still reeling from this second outburst when he explained that he'd just realised the time, and that he should by now be home with bib and feeding cup. But then it wasn't so bad. Monday was casserole; it would keep.

Would you believe it if I hadn't told? You see, there are people whose lives are that organised, and you don't just read about them in books; well, perhaps *you* do.

He thought he had better ring his mother; and did.

It gave me the chance to re-assess how things had gone. Completely out of control. The first part had worked a treat and my brilliant People Watching bit with him sizing up our Pam, then coming face-to-face; well, it's the sort of thing you dream about. Least I do. But somehow, somewhere along the trail, another Brenda had taken the controls and here she was lining up another date with this five-star wally. It was no use kidding that it was to spite Pam and her, 'Brenda can't keep a fella' wail. No, Pam had now met him, she'd sussed him, she even knew his bike had a bloody sidecar, so what was happening? What was this other Brenda up to?

I decided to climb up on the picture rail and watch. After all, if you suddenly find you're schizo it's no use worrying. You may as well enjoy it. Two lives are better than none.

He came back from the phone.

'OK?' I heard this other Brenda say.

'Yes. She worries when I'm out. You know what mothers are like.'

'Yes, I think so. Aren't they the ones with two bumps on the front?'

43

And right away I knew that me and the other Brenda weren't all that different.

'How is she then?' she went on.

'Oh, quite chirpy,' said Malcolm, and B2 and me pictured her pecking at the millet. 'She was telling me that Beethoven has just caught his first leaf.'

I watched B2 struggling not to say something devastating. She bit her lip and thought bland. 'Why Beethoven?' she asked.

'He was born the night we went to a concert at the Phil,' he explained.

'And they were playing Beethoven?' B2 reasoned.

'No, it wasn't actually,' he said, 'but you can't call a kitten Shostakovitch.'

B2 and me had a short conference. I was all for leaving there and then but she wanted to press on.

She pressed. 'Tell me, Malcolm, do you always have casserole on a Monday?'

'Always.'

'Tuesday?'

'Pork chop.'

'Nice.'

'Unless,' he added, 'Christmas day falls on a Tuesday.'

'Right,' she said. We all paused and thought, then, 'Turkey?' she asked.

'Right,' said Malcolm. And I nearly fell off the picture rail.

It was time to send B2 back to the co-pilot's seat.

I let him know gently that even if he wasn't hungry I was. So he offered to buy me a packet of crisps and if it hadn't been for B2 putting a restraining hand on my tongue the pleasantries would have ended there and then.

'I'd like something to *eat*,' I explained.

He suggested Indian which, as there's a great Tandoori just round the corner from The Grapes, was probably about the most intelligent thing he'd said since birth. Then he had second thoughts remembering that Pamela had said that she and Cloughie

44

were going for an Indian. I could see that he was
worried about being confronted by, and being caught
in, a Boston Crab. Fortunately at this point B2 took
over and consoled him saying that it was all a joke. As
he was still apprehensive she suggested we go Chinese
instead.

'I'd sooner not,' he said.

'You don't like Chinese?' asked B2.

'Love it,' he said. 'It's Indian I don't like. Can't
stand hot things.'

We puzzled.

'Then why did you suggest Indian?' we chorused.

'Well, *you* can eat, and I won't be tempted. Then I'll
still have room for my casserole.'

This was too much even for B2. We just sat there,
our joint flabber completely gasted.

'I can sit and nibble a poppadom,' he said.

CHAPTER TWELVE

The youngster who had been looking after my bike
wanted two pounds for his services. I thought this
was a bit steep and was prepared to make a lesser offer
when Brenda stepped in.

'You been demanding money for looking after
vehicles?'

'Only this one,' he said. 'The fellow with the flat tyre
just told me to sod off.'

I could see no sign of a flat tyre on the vehicle he
alluded to and when I mentioned this to Brenda she
said: 'He means later.'

All very confusing.

She told the youngster that he should come with us
and continue his minding service at the restaurant.
He didn't argue. You don't with Brenda.

The journey was a little odd. Brenda would not ride in the sidecar and of course as she had no helmet it would have been illegal for her to ride on the back. So she walked and I drove in first gear alongside her. The youngster had no such reservations about the sidecar and completed the journey standing and saluting the passersby like a general in one of those old war-time newsreels. I was glad it wasn't far.

I don't know whether I enjoyed the meal or not. At least I know *I* didn't enjoy a meal because I didn't have one; just three poppadoms, one of which was ruined by Brenda putting something hot on it when I turned away. Nearly blew the top of my mouth off. Rather infantile really. But otherwise it was quite pleasant. I told her about living in Chorley and then moving to Meols and about our previous cat Placido and about the Thurstaston Ornithological Society. She yawned once or twice but explained that that was simply because she'd hardly slept the night before because of the noise Pamela makes doing her weight training.

She then told me something of her background and it was amazing how we seemed to differ in every possible respect. Suppose I am bit of a loner. All my hobbies are rather solitary and I'm happy with just my own company. But she's got hundreds of friends and lives a really wild life. Some of the things she gets up to just defy description. And she has a very close knit family. Her mother was terribly upset when she flew the nest to live with her sister.

She talked some more of Pamela and her relationship with her boss (very complicated) and speculated that she was then probably flat on the canvas ready for her first submission. It struck me at the time as being a very catty thing to say, but in a way it typified Brenda in that she would say anything for a cheap laugh. I was beginning to doubt if Pamela had ever wrestled in her whole life.

'How long have you been a horni-whatsit?' she said.

She meant ornithologist. When I worked it out it

was close on fifteen years. Leonard had been a keen naturalist at school and although we weren't particular friends before, we sort of palled up about the time I got my first motorbike. We would go all over the place at weekends and in the holidays. Cheshire, North Wales and sometimes up to the Lakes. Leonard would navigate; I tend to get lost on my own. Mere Sands Wood up by Rufford was another favourite. Had my first kingfisher there; well, Len pointed it out. Odd thing is that I'm still not terribly good at it, whereas Leonard, well, as I said to Brenda: 'If there's a razorbill between here and Chester he'll spot it. Then he rings to tell me, but by the time I get there I'm either too late or the weather's turned lousy.'

She speculated that he might be just 'posing' as she called it.

'Maybe he hasn't seen it really,' she said. 'Mind, you wouldn't want to argue with someone called Razor Bill.'

That really made me laugh.

'No,' I said, 'the razorbill's a bird. My pal's Leonard.' Then I remembered. I glanced down at my wrist.

'Leonard!' I said.

'Is he in your watch?' she asked. But this was no time for flippancy. I was supposed to be picking him up at eight-thirty and it was already quarter past. I did my best to explain to Brenda but she made no effort to understand. I called the waiter but she was piqued and said: 'You go. Just leave me ten pence for your poppadom.'

Obviously I couldn't do that. After all, I had asked her out to eat; I think.

Then she was gone.

I paid and collected my things together, but by the time I reached the door there was no sign of her. A moody madam, my mother would have said. I felt slightly annoyed. In fact quite annoyed. Well, fairly annoyed. I obviously couldn't let Leonard down – anybody could see that. But she flounced off without

so much as a, ''Thank you for the meal, see you again,'
or even, 'I won't see you again.' And really that would
have been the best thing all round.

I drove slowly away turning back into the road that
passes The Grapes so that I could get my bearings
again. Then I saw her, clip-clopping on those silly high
heels. But there was no point in stopping. Then the
sidecar hood rattled and I had to.

The bike minder had settled himself in there and
dozed off. As I paid him I saw Brenda stop and stare.
Perhaps I should have said something. But what?
Two miserable ends to two miserable meetings. There
was no way either of us would want to risk a hat trick
by going to Buxton.

CHAPTER THIRTEEN

He drove past me and stopped. I stopped. I waited.
He opened the sidecar top. I thought, no chance. Then
the kid got out.

B2 gave me a sly inner look, but I didn't care. I told
her it saved me the trouble of telling him where to go.
What do you think this is, the Jackie Annual? And
that was that, and it was home to normal.

I went to a disco the next night and met up with Jan
and Paula. When Jan went to the loo Paula told me
what a bitch she was, and when Paula went Jan told
me what a bitch she was. By eleven o'clock I was
bursting.

Then they copped off with two school boys who'd
left their caps at home and I was stuck in the corner
minding the handbags. I didn't even have B2 to
telepath with. She hates discos; prefers music.

Funny how your mind wanders. All that noise, the
flashing neons, the ultra v. that makes your bra show
through, and what was I thinking about? Burton

bloody Marsh and that hawk thing flying round the copse. Stupid.

We got the last bus home and there was a nark between two scallies over who was staring at who. Then this skinny girl in a black leather mini was sick all over her boy friend. Oh yes, it was great to be back to normal.

When I got in Pam was in deep zizz. There was a note by the phone with a number to ring. I didn't recognise it. Couldn't think how the Meols Mackerel had got our number, unless he'd tried every Wilson P. in the book. Serve him right. I decided that I would, after delayed consideration, reluctantly accept an apology, provided it was abject enough.

The next morning I called, and they told me I owed £2.56 in library fines.

The day was already a drag. I had a chat with B2 and somehow we got round to the subject of the Mackerel. We decided that as drips go he'd run Niagara a close second. (Perhaps I should send my cousin a postcard of him.)

So why I should go to the shop that afternoon was a bit of a puzzle to both of us. Anyway, like I said before, I was bored, and I'd never been to Buxton, and I could borrow a helmet, and fresh air's good for you, and if you really want a reason pick one of those.

But it was probably Pam's fault.

She'd been on again about me not being able to keep a fellow long enough for his dandruff to settle and I told her she kept them so long the dandruff was encrusted on the pillow. Her pillow. But I was niggled. Perhaps it was because he didn't bite back. Didn't get annoyed; well, not sort of real annoyed like wanting to belt something, someone. Or perhaps I was just curious. Yes, that's probably it.

So I put on a pair of sunglasses and my posh frock that I'd got for my cousin Lynda's wedding that never happened because they decided to take the twins to Alicante instead, and I called at Waring's.

49

Malcolm was serving and didn't notice me come in so I went up to McManager. If he recognised me from the previous visit it didn't show. I put on my best Crosby Hairdresser voice and asked to see his braces. This earned just an eyelid's worth of confusion before he composed and said they'd got a very good range.

'Do you ride it or cook on it?' I asked, which at least earned a sneer and an attempt to pass me on to a minion.

'Terence at lunch?' he sniffed.

Malcolm had just reached that tricky bit where they put your plastic in a machine and iron it.

'Yes, Mr Ambrose,' he said, and looked up just as I was indicating to McManager the type of braces I wanted by twanging his. Magic!

Clocking me, Malcolm registered mega shock and with a great follow through on the ironing action knocked this tower block of boxed shirts off the counter and halfway across the shop.

Like I've said before, the best ones aren't planned. They just happen.

McManager was not amused and sounded off at poor Malcolm like a punctured bagpipe before mincing away to answer an off-stage phone. Malcolm blushed defiantly and puckered a lower lip . Once his customer was gone I helped pick up the boxes. I suppose it's possible that about this time either B2 or me had a twinge of something that might have been conscience. But it was probably wind.

Conscience isn't something we'd ever suffered with before.

CHAPTER FOURTEEN

The days were settling back into that repetitive blur where you can't remember whether it was a week last Tuesday you cut your toenails or the Tuesday before that. I stick to Tuesdays because it's easier after a bath. Other days I have a shower in the morning and I'm always pushed for time.

At the shop, business was getting worse. We open six days and have a day off each in turn, except for when one of us is on his two weeks annual, in which case we work the six and get days in lieu when the other comes back, though really it should be overtime, but the firm's in such a bad way that if you complained it would be cards on Friday. Fact is, there's seldom enough to keep two of us busy let alone three.

It was therefore, to all intents and purposes, just another day. Terry was on late lunch and I had just sold this chap a shirt with complimenting tie, ready boxed. He had looked at at least twenty, then chosen the first one I'd shown him. I knew he would; he was definitely the beige and mauve type. He'd also talked vaguely of a made-to-measure double breasted and I'd shown him some materials but then he said he'd leave it. I guessed he'd be Visa.

We were at the L-shaped counter in the centre of the store, and I was vaguely aware that behind me and to my left Ambrose was serving a posh young lady in a dress. (*She* was wearing the dress.) He spoke and I turned. Now I'm sure that the shock of seeing Brenda tugging at their boss's braces would make absolutely anybody knock over a stack of boxed shirts and a pattern swatch. Especially if they knew Brenda. Still, I don't suppose she meant it. Well, how could she? You can't *intend* to shock somebody into knocking over a stack of boxed shirts (and a pattern swatch). Anyway, I quickly regained my composure and gave Ambrose a withering look when he started in with the sarcastic comments. He made some excuse and went off to the stock room.

Brenda looked very attractive. I was glad Terry wasn't there.

She said she had popped in to confirm that we were going to Buxton on Thursday, my day off. Actually this came as something of a surprise *vis-à-vis* our last encounter but I reasoned that I must have misunderstood things. I vowed there and then to re-read my book on body language. She was very chatty and friendly, though she did intimate rather forcibly that she had no intention of riding in the Goldfish Bowl, as she called it, and would be borrowing a helmet from her sister. This intention was to have far greater consequences than either of us could ever have imagined at that time. For a start, had she been in the sidecar there would have been no room for the Welsh dresser. But I'm getting ahead of myself.

I said I'd pick her up just round the corner from The Grapes at half-nine. She needed time to get her sister off to work and do the washing-up and a few chores in the flat. Apparently Pam is very untidy and a lot falls on Brenda.

Then she went. When Ambrose came back he asked if she had bought a pair of braces. I laughed inwardly and told him she hadn't.

That night I got home to find my mother had other plans for my Thursday off. I knew something had upset her by the way she had skewered my corn on the cob, right through. All was soon revealed.

After many years of writing to Hugh Scully suggesting he bring his Antiques Roadshow to Meols, she had finally given up and asked the man from Caldwells in Chester to call round. His 'best offer' of sixty pounds for the Welsh dresser (less ten if they had to collect) merely added insult to injury. Foolishly I sympathised, and next I was agreeing to deliver the thing to save the tenner. Those of us possessed of a placid and easy-going disposition are frequently abused in this fashion. But I did wriggle.

I protested that I couldn't get the dresser in the sidecar, but she reminded me that that was precisely how we had got it from Aunty Blod's in Llanfairfechan a decade previous. So I then explained that I couldn't take it to Chester on the subsequent Thursday because I was meeting someone in Liverpool. This put the Inquisition on red alert.

Who was it? Did 'we' know her? Where precisely did she live, work, shop, have her hair done? Well, perhaps I exaggerate a little, but you can get the drift. I managed to not answer most, being much aided by my reputation for vacuousness. Finally she suggested that Brenda come round for tea. For the second time that day I enjoyed an inward chuckle. Fat chance.

Back to the matter of the Welsh dresser; my reasoned resistance was finally breached when she remembered that Caldwells have a branch in Liverpool. I could deliver it there prior to my assignation, as she called it.

As things turned out assassination would have been far more appropriate.

CHAPTER FIFTEEN

It was a lovely day. I ate a hearty breakfast which was significant I suppose, because you know who else eats a hearty breakfast, and as I washed up I gazed out of our back window. On the small piece of garden below, which everybody in the block claims not to be responsible for, some heavy-weight starlings were fighting over a piece of crust. I thought of Pamela. Above was a clear, blue sky, fringed by just a few fluffy, puffy clouds. I thought of Malcolm. It was already quite warm so riding on the back of a motor cycle would be great. I thought of me. Yes, a lovely, lovely day.

It could only get worse.
And it did, rapidly.

As I left the flat I felt quite self-righteous. Not only had I remembered to put the milk back in the fridge, but I'd got a skid lid so that I could now ride on the back of the sewing machine without upsetting anyone's legal sensibilities. So it was not unreasonable for me to assume that a certain ageing wally would have disconnected the Goldfish Bowl and left it at home.

But when the wally in question is one Stoneway, M, president of the International League of Super Wallies then you can also expect that what you expect, is too much to expect. But no one could have expected the sight that greeted me at ten o'clock that morning. (I'd even got up early.)

Not only was the bowl still connected, it was occupied. And not by another fellow, with a view to some kinky threesome. Nor by another woman so that we could at least take turns listening to his philosophy lectures. No, tied down, in case it tried to escape, was a cupboard.

He said it was a Welsh dresser, which was probably true. Only people who can call a village by a name half a mile longer than the main street could possibly invent a piece of furniture six foot high with a base barely two foot square.

I should have gone home right away, or even sooner. But I didn't. I was just that bit curious to know why anyone who wasn't on day release from the funny farm would want to take a thing like that for a day out.

He explained that he'd been taking it to an antique shop in the city centre and when he got there it was closed for refurbishment. So I explained that there was no way I was going to play gooseberry to a butty box that would have been too big even for our Pamela. He explained that if he took it back home we'd have wasted half the day so I explained that that was tough titty.

54

So far it had been nothing but expecting and explaining. It was to finish with me exploding, and I suppose it served me right. Deep down inside I must have some secret weakness for getting involved with the brain dead.

So I stepped outside of me again and watched. There they were on that lovely day, B2 arguing and shaking her head, Malcolm whimpering and nodding his, and in the sidecar, silent and stupid, Cuthbert the Cupboard.

I still don't know how she lost.

CHAPTER SIXTEEN

Then it hit me. We could kill two birds with one stone. (Sounds awful coming from a member of the RSPB but it's just an expression.)

'What about Chester?' I said. 'There's a Caldwells' there.'

She said she didn't care if there were wishing wells, she wasn't going. But she came. You see, deep down inside, I seem to have this ability to charm women. I don't really know how I do it but it always works. Well, nearly always. I suppose it's just a gift.

So we headed for Chester. The compromise was that we stuck to country roads. She seemed to think that if people saw the sidecar with the dresser in it they would laugh. More fools they, I thought.

Of course we had to clear the town first, and we did get the odd odd look, perhaps even a cat call or two, but sticks and stones as they say; not that anyone threw anything. We also had to cross the Mersey somewhere, so I went out to Widnes and across the bridge there, which is hardly leafy but once clear of Runcorn it was possible to head out towards Delamere Forest. After a pleasant hour's drive through the winding Cheshire lanes, with a bright sun flickering through the intermittent canopy of trees, I realised that we were, to all intents and purposes, lost.

Brenda was not amused. Arriving at a 'T' junction I consulted the map but was disappointed to find that there were quite a number of 'T' junctions in that particular quarter of O.S.117.

Then the bikers arrived. Three of them, one on a Harley Davidson. Greasy, grubby types, the sort who give us serious motorcyclists a bad image. I stared hard at the map. They circled a couple of times making childish remarks about the dresser.

Now I would have been happy to ignore them but Brenda derives some tribal pleasure from exchanging obscenities with their ilk. And I must admit she does happen to fare rather well in any insult trading competition. As they drove off she gave the greasiest of them instructions to get his face restudded, which would have been most satisfying, had it been the last we ever saw them.

Our Tour de Cheshire meant that we eventually arrived in Chester just in time to see Mr Flipping Caldwell turning his little cardboard sign over and going for his lunch. But no hassle. We stopped for ours.

Chester has these lovely old buildings with shops on two levels, so with an hour to kill it seemed sensible to find a spot on the upper tier and watch the world go by.

Have you noticed that a lunch hour always seems a lot less than sixty minutes when it's yours, and a lot more when it's somebody else's? I said as much to Brenda as I poured two beakers of decaffeinated from the flask and then added the milk. (It's better if you can carry it separately.)

As we tucked into my mother's rather special cheese and chutney sandwiches I elaborated further on the subject of time, as a catalogue of incidents, rather than just the number of beats made by a precision-made measuring instrument. She looked hard at me whilst she digested the concept.

As we shared a Kit Kat I proceeded to explain my philosophy. Well, one of them. I don't think she was at that juncture ready for determinism. This was more my general philosophy. You see, my *philosophie général*, as the French might say, is to be philosophical. OK, so half the day was lost. But a glass that is half empty is a glass that is half full. It's all a question of attitude. She frowned slightly and I took the opportunity to expand further. It was about this time that she, quite deliberately and for no apparent reason, took a half sausage roll and dropped it into my coffee.

Very odd.

CHAPTER SEVENTEEN

We'd been waiting three weeks for the stupid shop to open when Malcolm suddenly said, 'I'll take your picture.'

I wondered if it was for a passport so that we could head back to civilisation.

'Come on,' he said.

'Why?' I said.

' 'Cos,' he said. Well, he's into philosophy, you see.

So I sat on the wall, like he told me to, and I took off the helmet and put it down beside me like he told me to, and I sat a bit further back like he told me to, and knocked Sandra's helmet off and it landed on the back of a passing lorry.

So it was but definitely his fault.

I explained this at some length until I finally ran out of adjectives for him, his bike, his sidecar and his Welsh dresser. Sandra had not been keen to lend me the thing in the first place, her not having a sense of humour. Things had been a bit difficult from some time after I asked the handbag if he modelled gear for Action Man. But I pleaded and wheedled and lied that I thought he was a great guy really. In the end I swung it by promising I'd tell Mum she stayed the night at our place, next time I got a phone call on the subject. And now I'd lost her helmet. She'd be livid, and would go on about it for centuries. Some people do, don't they.

During one of the times when I stopped for breath the shop opened and we got rid of Cuthbert. Malcolm then came very close to death when he said that in one respect it had worked out OK as although I hadn't got a helmet, there was now room for me in the sidecar. In fact, execution was only stayed when he swore hand on kidney that he would buy a replacement helmet for Sandra the next day. And anyway, I still had to get home.

So we left Chester but under new rules, the first being that I would not travel in the Bowl for more than fifteen minutes at a time.

First stop was a café. We went in.

The run had given me chance to recharge my ranting batteries and I was still going strong when who should roll in but the three chimpanzees we'd met earlier. The troop leader was blond and not too ugly, but the other grease balls shared a dose of acne left over from the plague.

They did the hard case entrance bit so that everybody in the café looked at them and pretended not to.

At the counter they ordered three pints of bitter and a bag of oats for the horse, and were given three Cokes. They spotted us and came across.

'Look who it is,' said Blondie, 'Batman and Robin.'

'Go away,' I told him, 'you'll curdle the milk.'

Malcolm's head tortoised downwards into his leathers.

'Oh aye, cheeky with it,' said Very Spotty.

'Still doing furniture removals?' said Even Spottier.

'Yes,' I said, 'and nose removals, so beat it.'

For a while I gave as good as, with interest, but

Malcolm frowned and continued to shrink into his jacket until all that was left showing was his hair and a half inch of wrinkled forehead.

'Little Robin Redbreast *is* a tough one, isn't she?' said Blondie.

'How do you know what colour they are?' said Very Spotty. 'What do you reckon, Batman? Has Robin got red . . . ?'

But I interrupted and told him which part of his anatomy I was about to redden with my boot.

At last Malcolm spoke. Manfully he leapt to the defence of his damsel who was under attack from these three dragons who hadn't heard of Listerene.

'Brenda,' he said, 'hush.'

I was disgusted. Really disgusted. Looking back, I suppose in the circumstances a show of rampant cowardice was a reasonable strategy, but then, I was disgusted.

'Now, Robin, do as the Caped Crusader says,' Blondie went on.

I did. I stayed hushed and just stared my disgustedness at the lot of them.

I suppose the atmosphere did then come down a charge or two and they got to talking about bikes. They were interested in Malcolm's machine, it being vintage which means even older than him, and the sidecar which was mega interesting being older still, having been made from off-cuts from the Ark.

I cooled and dozed. Then the troop trooped off.

Malcolm said: 'Phew!'

I said: 'Dickheads.'

Oh maybe he was right not to bite, but I hate to let crap like that get the better of me. Still, it wasn't worth arguing about.

We had another coffee and for some reason I felt a bit better. Maybe I'd run my bile duct dry.

So we sat and looked at each other. And then I got one of those twingy feelings that I wasn't too sure about, so I got him talking about his bike. He told me that sometimes he had to make his own replacement engine parts and it might have been about this time that I thought that maybe he wasn't quite the wally he pretended to be, and maybe with a bit of, well, sort of house training, we might, you know. Twingies can make you think real dumb things, can't they?

'You're a deep one, Batman,' I said.

He smiled.

'Am I, Robin?'

And the helmet didn't matter, nor the chimps, nor even Cuthbert the Cupboard.

'Should we go back to the Batmobile?' he said.

And I said; 'Lead on, Caped Crusader.'

And ignored a lifetime's teaching that you should never drop your guard. Never stop thinking that people are horrible and devious and you should always expect the worst of them.

CHAPTER EIGHTEEN

With a little tact and diplomacy I had managed to defuse a rather dangerous confrontation with the three bikers. Of course we did share a common interest, and they were quite impressed, when I told them something of my machine's history. As we left the café we found them standing admiring it. The blond one helped Brenda into the sidecar and my apprehension that she would start again with the verbal fisticuffs proved unfounded.

With more than a touch of relief I kick-started (first time!) and accelerated away.

Even over the noise of my engine I could hear their hysterical baying. I stopped and turned to be met by the piercing gaze of Brenda in the sidecar. It was supported by three bricks under the joining bracket. As I took in the scene the bikers jumped on their machines and drove off, one of them making a rude gesture with the bolts they had removed.

There had been a moment in the café, just a moment, when I'd felt that Brenda and I, well, communicated. Before that, the day had been one of increasing aggro, and I resented the fact that the whole fault was placed at my door whereas, in fairness, I should have been assigned at most perhaps fifty percent. I suppose, therefore, that I should not have been surprised that the hysteria triggered by this latest incident should have been directed at me in its entirety. I helped her out of the sidecar.

'They disconnected it,' I explained.

'Even I know that,' she yelled. 'Just fix it and let's get the hell out of here. It's humiliating.'

I pointed out that they'd taken the bolts, whereupon she suggested I use the one from my neck. I took this to be some obscure Frankenstein allusion. She walked away.

I followed.

'Look, Brenda,' I said, 'I've another set in the garage at home. I can be there in fifteen minutes.'

She stopped, thought, sighed.

'OK, then. Let's go.'

I took a deep breath. It was necessary to remind her yet again that she couldn't come on the back of the bike, because she hadn't got a helmet. For no reason at all she then hit me very hard on the top of mine.

Leasowe Lighthouse was built in 1828 and has 650,000 bricks all made from clay dug from the land nearby. My mother is one of its Friends. At least she was then. Not now, because it's a club. They lost the fight to preserve it, you see.

Perhaps I should explain.

We live on the front at Meols on the end of the Wirral peninsular, and Leasowe Lighthouse is a couple of miles away, along the coast. Well, it would be, wouldn't it. There's not much call for lighthouses inland. In fact, there hasn't been much call for this one at all since 1925, but when a certain brewery wanted to take it over, my mother and her friends tried to stop them. They formed the 'Friends of Leasowe Lighthouse' and had meetings. 'So what?' you say. Well, I only mention this because there was such a meeting going on in our house when I got home to get the replacement bolts so that I could fix the sidecar back on, and take Brenda home. Clear?

Trouble was, my mother had had a 'big' tidy. She has tidies of varying sizes at far shorter intervals than needs must, and usually when 'people' are coming. And if one of those people should be Mrs Lloyd Roberts (and it was on this occasion because she was the then president of the Friends), you can guarantee that it will be a biggy. This involves turning out every drawer and cupboard in the house and rearranging and/or relocating all sorts of things that haven't been touched since the last big tidy. Things like the garage key. Now do you understand?

I had a quick search of the kitchen, trying all the usual places but no sign. The Friends' meeting was in full flow in the living room and I sidled in at the back. Someone had just proposed that they have a mass picket of the site. I tried to attract my mother's attention but she was busy explaining that she couldn't picket on the following Wednesday because she had the chiropodist.

So I went back to the kitchen and had another search, and a drawer jammed, and I got annoyed, and I pulled it very hard and it came out suddenly, and I knocked over a trifle which emptied onto a tray of tuna and cucumber baps. I shan't bore you with the row that followed. Suffice to say I eventually got the key and then the bolts. Trouble was that by the time I got back to the café I'd been away almost an hour. But I still thought she would have waited.

I went into the café and asked the bloke if he'd seen her.

'Are you Malcolm Stoneway?' he said, and when I

admitted I was, he presented me with a piece of rolled-up newspaper.

Inside were the bolts.

So now I had two sets. Seems they'd had a conscience about their pathetic trick after all. But how had they known my name?

I went out and was connecting up the sidecar again, when one of them drove past. He revved loudly and waved and catcalled before accelerating off in the direction of the motorway, just as the second one turned a nearby corner and did the same. I waited and sure enough along came the third. The blond one. He just grinned but the girl on the back didn't even look across.

It was Brenda.

CHAPTER NINETEEN

I got to The Grapes to find Pamela already planted. Really, I don't know why I tell her things. She's never sympathetic. But you've got to tell someone, and she is, besides being my sister, my best mate. Well, my only mate really. No, that's not true. I've lots of mates but I just can't be bothered keeping up the contacts. People can be so touchy, can't they? One minute it's all pals together and taking the piss out of one another, and the next they've gone huffy and are talking about you behind your back and going places and not telling you. Not that I'd want to go anyway. Of course I can always chew things over with B2 but too much of that and they lock you up.

Pam slid along the seat a bit so that I could join her. Three people fell off the other end.

'Good day?' she asked.

I explained how it had started as a good day. A

great day even, but then it had plummeted faster than Kajagoogoo's greatest hit.

'Would you believe that I went all the way to Chester on a heap of scrap iron, accompanied by a Welsh dresser and a Wirral plonker?'

'No,' she said.

'Or that our Sandra's helmet got stolen by a lorry?'

'No,' she said.

'Or that the Plonker finally drove off, leaving me sitting in his sidecar like a prize prune in Lewis's window?'

'That I believe,' she said.

There's a time to make smart-ass cracks and there's a time to be sympathetic. Pamela, being as sensitive as a varnished armadillo, though not as good-looking, always gets it wrong. I pressed on.

' "Back in half an hour," he said. Big joke.'

I explained about me then being offered alternative transport by a real biker on a real bike, and how this led to the final humiliation. I paused the way you do when you're being dramatic. Then told her: 'We were stopped by the fuzz, in Birkenhead.'

I paused again to give her chance to wonder why.

'Speeding?' she wondered.

I shook my head.

'Carrying excess baggage?' she smirked, cracking her varnish.

'We were stopped,' I explained, 'because I was not wearing a bloody helmet.'

And she laughed till the tears ran down her snout.

When she stopped for breath I told her I hoped her next termite hill would collapse on her, and left.

I never saw him again. Well, he lived over the water and I didn't go that way much. Then. Least I don't think I ever saw him again. Have you ever thought that somebody who you once knew briefly, a long time ago, might have been sitting near you in the pictures or gone past you in a shop, but because he's shaved off his beard or she's dyed her hair, or vice versa, you never noticed?

Must happen all the time. So maybe I have seen him again. Blondie, I mean. Sorry, did you think I was referring to the Meols' Mackerel? Oh, I've seen him again. And again. Though honest to God I've tried not to.

I managed a full week after the Chester débâcle. (Got that one from a crossword. Anagram of 'bed lace'. It's posh for cock up.)

A full week. Great, it was. Just like the old days. Up in time for Thomas the Tank Engine. Afternoons reading, or writing letters to the *Echo* about young people swearing on escalators, signed, Disgusted of Knotty Ash. Then a mad dash before Pam gets in, and making a big mess in the kitchen so it looks as if I've been cooking since yesterday.

Evenings out – maybe a bit of People Watching. Then home to a little playful banter with my ever-loving sister as she sat taking extra shorthand from Mr Clough on the settee. I say banter but it was a bit one-sided. She tended to get fits of the sulks, but it wasn't my fault it was only a two-roomed flat, and what did she expect me to do; take a three hour bath? Anyway, she was never a good loser.

Then one morning I got up and it was like someone had left the fridge door open. I pretended not to notice.

'What time did old Cloughie leave then?' I chatted.

Silence.

'Never mind,' I pursued. 'Too many late nights might ruin your performance – at work that is.'

More frost.

'Course, it's a long trek home for him,' I pressed. 'Frodsham isn't it? Poor beggar. Fancy being a deputy assistant undermanager brackets claims, and on top of that having to live in Frodsham.'

'Shut up,' she chatted.

'Did you know that you can't get a house there unless you've got "O" level "Boring"?'

She curled a lip.

'Shut bloody up, or you'll feel my boot; at "A" level.'

Not bad considering she was out of practice.

'Pamela, is something up?' I innocented.

She repeated, this time at dictation speed: 'Shut – your – blabbering – face.'

'No,' I sympathised, 'because if there is something bothering you, I would want you to tell me.'

At this, the blue touch paper gave a final splutter and then, *bang!*

'You're the matter. You and your pathetic jokes and infantile behaviour.'

What a thing to say. Me, infantile! I told her that if that was her attitude I wouldn't lend her my nurse's outfit ever again. But she was not to be deviated – if you see what I mean.

'One more performance like last night and you are out,' she said. 'I can soon get someone else to share this flat.'

So that was what it was about.

'What did I do?' I lied.

'Last night, Sidney and I worked late . . .'

'Sidney,' I relished, 'you didn't tell me his name was Sidney.'

'We came back here with two chow mein and a bottle of dry white for a quiet evening to wind down. Then you come in with your: 'Oh hello, is this Mr Clough, or is this the other one?'

'Sorry, Pam,' I spanieled.

'You're not funny. Just a stream of school girl prattle, cheap jibes and old jokes. You go too far.'

I shrugged. She glared. I had to say something. 'But apart from that, Pam, is something bothering you?'

Whereupon she proved conclusively that going with the Frodsham Ferret had completely ruined her sense of humour by grabbing my hair and pushing me face first into a bowl of cornflakes.

Very childish.

66

CHAPTER TWENTY

At home, life continued in its comfortable rut. I might
have said boring rut, but recent events had taught me
how comfortable was comfortable. Occasionally little
blips of incident flickered on the oscilloscope of life
but nothing to necessitate a change of the 'Y' axis scale
factor. Not quite so at work, but I'll come to that.

There was the small blip triggered by Aunty Peggy's
wheelchair for instance.

Aunty Peggy, my mother's sister, suffers from
arthritis. But she's a tough old stick and, if truth be
known, a bit on the wild side. Odd how sisters can be
so different, though I *can* think of one other case!
Every now and again she has a crunch with the chair
and guess-who is called in as chief mechanic to do the
repairs. If it was a car she'd never even get to ten
percent with her no claims bonus.

Peggy lives with Uncle Bernard in Aigburth, a
suburb in the south end of Liverpool, so if there's a job
to do I usually go straight from work. This I did one
Thursday – the Thursday I bought the helmet –
the Thursday I met Sidney – the Thursday I first
heard of the rodent fixation and the geranium
problem. Oddly it wasn't a bad Thursday for me. For
others it had a blip so big it must have gone right off
the tube. But here I go racing ahead again. Let's go
back a bit. Say to Wednesday.

Being a fan of predestination has its good side. With
any other philosophy I might have felt that the Brenda
visitation was somehow self-induced. But I knew what
it happened because it had to happen. Maybe it was to
make a better man of me – or a worse one. Who can
say? And *do* we learn from our experiences? You might
say yes, but think of the number of times you've made
the same mistake(s) over again. Does a series of
misunderstandings, embarrassments, disasters leave
a mark? Was I, in the period immediately A.B. (After

Brenda, as I thought it then was), more pragmatic? Hardly. More phlegmatic? Possibly. More wary? Definitely. And does it matter? *Que sera, sera*, as we determinists say.

So, to Wednesday and the shop. A peaceful week had slipped by and I was happy to let the Brenda interlude fade into the haze of distant hauntings. But Terry wasn't. During the days immediately A.B. he quizzed and wormed and eventually got the whole story from me. Of course it was all my fault.

'Any floss would get hostile with a bloke who brings a wardrobe on a date.'

I didn't bother to point out that it was, in fact, a Welsh Dresser. He'd have said I was being pedantic – except that I doubt he knows the word.

'She sounds a bit of all right this Brenda,' he said. 'You just haven't been handling her properly.'

I guessed this was the prelim to some coarse prescription but he went on: 'What's missing is a bit of romance.'

When I realised that he was serious I was amazed. This, from the original wham, bam and thank you mam, of Hemel Hempstead.

'You should buy her a present,' he said.

It was hopeless. I just could not get through to him.

'Look,' I said. 'Each of our meetings finished progressively higher on the Richter Scale of Catastrophes. I just do not want another.'

'I'll have a word,' he said.

'No,' I said. And refused to co-operate when he asked me to describe her. Why he was so persistent in wanting to meet her and fix things up for me I simply could not understand.

But he remembered that I said they went to The Grapes, and that they usually sat by the space invaders machine.

CHAPTER TWENTY-ONE

I went out with the very best of intentions, I swear I did. It's true, honest. May I fall off this wardrobe if I'm telling a lie. And Cloughie had just rung. You see, I'd got this lousy dose of conscience over ruining Pam's evening with him and I was determined to make it up to her. Anyway, I hate it when we're not speaking. And it's worse for me. At least she has people in the office to talk to. The best I can hope for is the chance to warn Thomas the Tank Engine that there's a snow drift round the next bend. And he never takes any notice.

So on this Wednesday I went out and just happened to be passing our bus stop at quarter to six when she just happened to be getting off her usual bus.

'Hi,' I said in my best what-a-coincidence voice.

She didn't answer so I walked alongside her and prattled as if she had. Then I managed to steer her into The Grapes on the promise of me paying. I suppose the novelty must have appealed to her lesser nature. and when I set them up she almost said thanks. But I did have a make-her-talk card up my jumper.

'Cloughie rang just as I was coming out,' I said. 'From Birmingham.'

'Oh,' she said. She was weakening.

'He'd tried the office but you'd just left.'

I then stayed quiet for a while to make her ask, but she didn't. She'd played before.

'He said to tell you that he's working late and will be there till seven if you want to ring him.'

She flicked a frown at me that said: 'If you're making this up I'll chop you into bite-sized pieces and feed you to the fishes.'

She has a very extensive line in frowns, being something of a wrinkly before her time. I swore truth, so off she went to the phone in the other bar with a fist full of my ten pence pieces and no promise to repay because she still wasn't really speaking.

And there I was, sitting, supping, musing, while she

was away whispering sweet nothings at the Frodsham
Ferret and longing for the day he'd be back, which
turned out to be Thursday, or tomorrow as it then was.
Then in mid-muse I heard: 'Is your name Brenda?'

I looked up to see this bloke with spiky hair and suit
to match standing over me. He looked vaguely
familiar.

'No,' I said, 'is yours?'

Well, you would, wouldn't you? I mean anyone
more than a fortnight out of nappies knows that rule
one is 'Don't admit to anything'. My dad told me it's
even in the AA Handbook.

'Oh,' he said, and turned to the space invader
machine. I explained gently that playing it before 11
pm was a knee-capping offence seeing as how it got on
my nerves. He tried sarky and said he'd take it through
to the other room only it was bit heavy; so I suggested
he made two journeys. He stared hard at me.

'You sure you're not Brenda?' As if it was something that most people were in doubt about some
time in their lives.

Then it happened; a flash. It's really brilliant when
one sentence, one inspired phrase even, can set you
off on a scam better than the best you could ever
dream up, given sixth months' dreaming time and
your own joke shop.

'I've a sister called Brenda,' I said.

He stared even harder, and then I remembered
where I'd seen him. He was the poser from Waring's.
All began to fall into place as he went on:

'It's just that I've a mate. Chap I work with, and he
says this girl he knew called Brenda usually sits
here – by the space invader machine. My name's
Terry Milton.'

Perhaps I should have sympathised but I've heard
worse names.

'Mind if I sit down?' he went on.

I asked if this mate of his was one Malcolm Bird-
brain Stoneway and when he said it was I told him I
did mind. Then he played detective.

70

'You're Pamela, aren't you?'

I had already decided that I was, this being stage two of the earlier mentioned inspired scam.

'I thought you'd be bigger,' he said.

I explained that I was on a diet and asked him if Malcolm had mentioned that I used to wrestle for Bootle.

'He thought that was just a joke,' he said.

I denied hotly.

'Fact is our Brenda and me have decided to become a "tag team". She's on the phone to Sidney Clough right now.'

He looked puzzled.

'Surely you've heard of Big Sid?' I said. 'Biggest name in wrestling in all of Frodsham.'

When he admitted that he'd never even heard of Frodsham having only moved north six months ago I explained what a depraved place it was, and that if they ever did a telly series there it would make Miami Vice seem like Trumpton. He seemed interested and I was about to tell him where to catch the bus when he harked back to Brenda. Instinct told me that the scam would fizzle if they met this early, so I advised him to move on before she got back as she was still pretty hostile towards his mate Malcolm and he might cop an earful by association.

'Oh, but I'm not like him,' he said. 'I wouldn't take a Welsh Dresser on a date. Might take an undresser though.'

He certainly fancied his chance. I said how lucky it was for us females that there were fellows like him around and hoped he wouldn't jam his head in the doorway on the way out.

He went back to the bar and sulked into a pint.

Pam came back. She was now all bright-eyed and bushy, just like someone who had been chatting to her lover boy and planning a nosh for two in the flat for the following evening when he got back from Birmingham, and, by an amazing coincidence, she had.

Seems he would be telling a certain relation by marriage that he wouldn't be back until much later than, etc., which would give more time for the other. The other continued to beam.

All this Mills and Booning was giving me gullet problems so to change the subject I suggested some People Watching. Pam didn't really want to know, saying that she was very tired and wanted a bath and an early night in that order. I worried that if it was having this effect on her it must be killing Cloughie. I told her to go easy with him as we didn't want anything happening at our place as it would be hell getting a stretcher down the stairs. She said I was sick, which was true, and she would have left there and then had I not been inspired to point out a Newy.

A Newy is someone in The Grapes we've not seen before, and as you might guess they have a certain scarcity value. As confirmed People Watchers we treasure them. So I offered Pam first shot at Terry the Treasure.

She did not make a very impressive start.

'Bit of a Trendy Wendy,' she said. 'About twenty-six; from Crosby. Works in an office, in accounts.'

I dozed off loudly.

'OK, OK,' she said, 'But at weekends he hangs out with the Waterloo and District Nude Hang Gliding Club.'

Well, I suppose he would. Then it was my turn.

I guessed he was from Hemel Hempstead (thanks to M) and that he ran a protection racket for the local massage parlour; hobbies were playing travel scrabble on his exercise bike and collecting antique plastic bin liners.

Now normally it doesn't matter who's right – just whose ideas are the craziest, but I wanted to see her face when she found that, by an amazing coincidence, my guess as to his roots was correct – the craziest guess of all you might think, but on the other hand somebody has to come from Hemel Hempstead.

What's more I was ready for stage three. I challenged Pam to chat him up and find out who was nearest. She was not inclined, so I introduced a little needle to her tender regions by suggesting her reluctance was because she was saving herself for Sidney. I added that she shouldn't think like that, as I was sure he sometimes cheated on her, and slept with his wife. She glared fondly and gave my carotid artery a playful squeeze, but in the end accepted the dare. Well, just because you're past twenty doesn't mean you've got to behave like it. I suggested the 'tap his elbow with your drink' technique, even though it had backfired more than badly on me just a Malcolm ago. Or maybe because it had.

So she went up behind him and tapped, but nothing happened. They must breed them with thick elbows in Hemel Hempstead.

'Harder,' I mouthed.

So she did. And he turned suddenly and she got best part of a pint of bitter down her frock.

Magic!

See what I mean? How could anyone have planned that?

My first instinct was to follow a dripping sister from the pub but then I had a second, reasoning that until she came down a dudgeon or two I might be apportioned some blame for the dousing. She can be very illogical where I'm concerned. As the earlier thaw had hardly started it was definitely best to give time for things to settle and clothing to at least reach the rinse cycle.

Terry came across, eager to explain.

'That was Brenda, was it? I'm sorry, but she jogged my elbow.'

Rule twenty-seven says that when on a winning streak don't stop. Or is it twenty-six? Anyway, I put on 'serious and concerned' and said: 'It's the frock. She's got an interview tomorrow for a job. Lime Street. As a station announcer. She's been practising for months now with three conkers in her mouth and her head in a bucket.'

73

Don't know that he bought that, but he wasn't sure about the dress.

'Hasn't she got another?' he asked.

At this point I shed the third stage and went into orbit.

'None that fit. She's put on a stone in the last month. Can't stop eating. It's her complaint, you see. It goes in cycles.'

'What complaint?' he panicked.

I pretended not to hear.

'I'll have to get back soon. It's times like this, when she's upset, that she forgets to take her tablets.'

'Brenda?' he said.

'Yes?' I said, then covered quickly when I remembered who I was. 'What about her?'

'What are the tablets for exactly?'

'Her metabolism,' I said. 'Without them it gets unstable.'

'What happens?'

'It falls over,' I reasoned. Then pressed on, high on inspiration: 'Can be very embarrassing. When we visit friends I always ring first to remind them to hide their geraniums.'

He believed me, I know he did. I was just so good, I even convinced myself.

'Why?' he said.

'Brenda eats them,' I explained. 'See, when it gets really bad she thinks she's a hamster.'

'Malcolm didn't mention any of this,' he puzzled.

'He wouldn't know. As long as she takes the tablets she's OK.'

He nodded understanding and I risked all by adding: 'Occasionally she puffs out her cheeks but you wouldn't think anything unless you knew.' Then stood up to go before he could flicker doubt. 'See you.'

'Just a minute,' he said.

I froze. OK, so I had pushed it too far. I waited as his brain creaked into second gear. He frowned his suspicion.

'Do hamsters eat geraniums?'

'Well, she's not really a hamster, is she?' I pointed out. And somehow this seemed to make sense of the whole thing.

He put his hand on my arm. 'Pamela.'

'Yes?' I said, still a bit wary.

'What are you doing tomorrow?'

This did catch me out I must admit, and I was even more surprised to hear me say I'd be outside the Odeon at seven.

As I left I wondered if I would be.

CHAPTER TWENTY-TWO

Terry's description of events at The Grapes the night before was quite entertaining. The image of Brenda copping a full pint had great appeal, particularly as I guessed she'd been trying the 'drink against the elbow' routine, which she had once worked on me. However, I didn't convey my suspicion to Terry. He'd have resented my not warning him. He did express surprise at my patent delight and said it wasn't like me to be malicious. This was true, but I told him I was happy to make an exception in her case. As is the way of things, subsequent revelations left me feeling considerable guilt regarding the release of these baser instincts, but initially I relished the image of her squelching soggily from the pub.

He also told me that Brenda had a job interview which came as something of a surprise though now I can't think why. However, the thing that gave me amazement maximus was the news that Terry was taking Pam to the pictures that evening.

You see, deep down, I'd suspected that his motive in going to The Grapes was not altogether altruistic, and that under the guise of putting things straight between Brenda and me he was really looking to chance his own arm. My reasoning was simple enough. Terry does quite fancy himself as a ladies' man – not without cause I must add – and my description of Brenda might well have whetted his appetite. Something of a challenge perhaps. But I'd been wrong and it was Pam he had taken to.

He remarked that it was a pity I'd blown it with Brenda as we could have made up a foursome. The sheer horror of this prospect left me dumbstruck. This turned to complete confusion when he added that should I ever decide to make it up with Brenda and buy her a present, I should ensure that it wasn't a geranium. That's right. A geranium, and the reason was even more bizarre. In fact, I could hardly believe the tale of her unstable metabolism and hamsterine tendencies.

Then Terry moved away to serve a customer and I had time to think more deeply on all he had said. I recalled Brenda's references to the sidecar smelling of dead gerbils; perhaps some sort of rodent fixation? Maybe. In fact the more I thought of her and her unpredictable behaviour the clearer things became. She had always reached her most irrational after a long day out; evidently when she had failed to take her tablets. And why? Embarrassment. Yes, that was it. Brenda, cool, sharp, with it; to have been seen taking medication would have meant complete loss of face.

At this distance I can of course see the flaw in my reasoning. After all, she could have nipped out to the Ladies and taken them – but then, the thought didn't even cross my mind. Or perhaps it wanted to and couldn't.

That's the thing about predestination. I think it was Thomas Hobbes (1588–1679) who said, 'Hindsight may show us a myriad of alternatives but these are not visible as we plough the single furrow of our destiny.' Or perhaps it was me.

Then came the guilt. What had I done? M. Stoneway, tolerant, understanding, liberal to a fault (small 'l') had, when put to the test, condemned, despised, even gloated at the discomfort of someone who was stricken with metabolic instability. Giving her condition its full medical title made my behaviour seem even worse. I was glad to know it was controllable.

How sad to think we had never reached that plane of contact on which she would have felt free to confide.

What to do? Perhaps I could, should, make amends. Terry had mentioned a present.

A present, but not, of course, a geranium.

CHAPTER TWENTY-THREE

Like my uncle Bert said when he sub-let a corner of his allotment to my dad to grow hops, every plot has its price. The price I payed for what was probably the best plot since the time I got the school kitchen cleaned up in time for a surprise visit from the Public Health that never happened, was a date with Terry Milton.

Up to then the day had been fine. I'd been up at the crack of ten. Tried Pamela's new Body Shop Shampoo (five quid a bottle!). Advised Thomas how to hook on his new tender, and written seven pages to Canada. I'd then had a little chat with B2 who'd been feeling a bit left out. I explained that as I was currently an occasional Pamela she'd have needed to be an occasional P2 and then things really would have got complicated. She understood. Then I set off for the Odeon.

If I've given the impression that Terry is a bit of a big head I've misled you. He's a lot of a big head. You know the type. Think that they've been delivered on this earth Red Star, as some sort of Reader's Digest Bonus Award, for the benefit of the female population.

When I arrived the first thing he did was to look at his watch as if he didn't know it was ten past seven, this being, as you now know, for me, the equivalent of early. Then he *tells* me that we are going for a coffee to kill some time and will come back in half an hour to catch the complete performance on Screen Four. *I* might have already seen it. *I* might have wanted to do something else; like, well, I can't think of anything at the moment but I might have then. But no. Terence had spoken. Screen Four it was. And if he hadn't said: 'Right, this way, *Pam*,' I could easily have elbowed him there and then. But I needed that little reminder of who I was, and why.

Over coffee I got a detailed breakdown of the delights of Hemel Hempstead, chief of which is apparently a very large roundabout. I yawned my amazement as he then moved on to his inevitable progression to the dizzy heights of shop management and the changes he would make that would rock the foundations of the whole retail world. By comparison, the Meols Mackerel was a barrel of laughs.

On top of everything the film was crap. Just as well I was Pamela watching it and not me, or I'd have walked out.

We arrived back at the flat to find her and Cloughie so entangled on the settee that when they separated they were wearing each other's sweaters. Pam was not pleased.

'What the hell are you doing here?' she yelled over the whirr of closing zips.

'Making amends,' I explained, 'I'm going to make supper for you both,' and I went through to the kitchen. She followed, still fastening.

'Coffee?' I said.

'No,' she screamed.

'Two teas then?' I reasoned, and reached for the milk, only for her to snatch it from me. Why I don't know. Maybe she felt I was intruding, but there was no chance to ponder this as my light grip and her powerful pull resulted in one jug's worth of semi-skimmed being deposited down her front. If this was just a story you'd say, 'Oh no. Not two days running.'

And rightly. But this was life and a person *can* get two pints down two frocks on two consecutive days. I consoled and ushered her through to the bathroom. She didn't say much. She couldn't, and fortunately I've never learnt to lip read.

Back in the living room our two male guests, for want of a better expression, were getting on confusedly. I told them the coffee wouldn't be long and returned to the kitchen so that I could earwig at the door. They had evidently swopped names and Terry recognised the other.

'From Frodsham?' he asked.

Apprehensively Cloughie admitted he was.

'You'll be Big Sid then,' said Terry. 'The wrestling promoter?'

Cloughie denied hotly.

'Who told you that?' he pressed.

'Pamela,' said Terry.

'You know her?'

'Of course. Mind I only met her last night. She was telling me the problems she has with Brenda. Her needing medication.'

Cloughie said he wasn't surprised, which gave me another reason to hate him.

'I find her most odd,' he said.

'You've known her long?' asked Terry.

'Met her for the first time on Tuesday. Pam and I were enjoying a very pleasant evening till she breezed in.'

'You were here with Pam?' amazed Terry. And then confided that we seemed to be a very free and easy pair, emphasising the 'easy'.

The kettle boiled and I was able to take in the coffees before they started to put names to faces.

'She'll be out in a minute,' I said. 'Slight accident.'

'Has she taken her tablets?' enquired Terry.

'Tablets?' said Cloughie.

'Headache,' I said giving Terry a warning glare.

Unfortunately he seemed to be glareproof and pressed on conversationally: 'Did she get the job?'

Again the Frodsham Echo: 'Job?'

'Didn't go,' I said hurriedly and sent Terry to get some biscuits from the kitchen which I knew hadn't got any. Then things really started to move.

First Pam reappeared with an ominous: 'I want a word with you,' but before I could even finish putting on my injured innocence expression the phone rang. I picked it up and hid my face in the mouthpiece as Sidney accused his secretary of applying for another job and Pam accused her boss of speaking by other than the usual orifice.

And on the phone?

Malcolm, and my turn to be surprised.

'I've something for you,' he said.

'Like what?'

'A present.'

'Expensive?'

'What do you mean?'

'More than twenty?'

'Yes.'

Well, seeing as how things were boiling up nicely, and I've a weakness for presents worthy of the name, and I might need help to do a runner soon, and I had just been out with Terry, I managed to forget I had sworn never to see the Mackerel again, and said: 'Where are you?'

Shock two: 'Across the street,' he said. 'I've just been to my Auntie Peggy's to mend her wheelchair.'

So on top of everything he's Mother Teresa.

'Come up,' I said. 'There's no one here.' And rang off.

Pamela was staring.

'Who was it?'

'Just some woman,' I shrugged, 'Very insistent, but I told her there was no one here called Sidney.'

'What!' panicked Cloughie.

'Take no notice, she's sick,' Pamela said, having known me long enough.

'Has she taken her tablets?' Cloughie asked, not knowing me at all.

Terry reappeared and said: 'Can't find any.'

'Tablets?' said Cloughie.

'No, biscuits.'

'What tablets?' Pamela said.

'He said she was on tablets,' Cloughie said, looking at Terry.

Then the doorbell went and I nodded to Cloughie to dive under the table and he would have done if Pamela hadn't stopped him.

So I went to the door. And they were all shouting at each other.

Bliss!

CHAPTER TWENTY-FOUR

Buying the helmet was one thing (I kept the receipt just in case). Giving it to her was another. I mean, she is so unpredictable, and it was rather late. As I left Peggy's I'd decided the best course was to pop round with it the following day. Then I thought, 'What the hell, I'm passing.' And finally I'd compromised with the phone call; avoid the face-to-face – just in case. But she is, like I've said, so unpredictable. I was ready for a tentative, 'How are you? Weather's nice.', or even a, 'Who is it? Get lost', but 'Expensive? More than twenty?', well, that really caught me flat aback. Damn cheeky really. Even so I was still a touch apprehensive when I reached the front door.

I assumed she had the TV on rather loud as I could hear raised voices. Brenda ushered me in and I gave her the helmet. She was very pleased. Then she ushered some more and I found it wasn't the TV. There was Terry and Pamela and another chap! Some sixth sense told me who it was. Brenda confirmed: 'This is Sidney Clough,' she said. Wow, Pamela's boss. He must have caught her with Terry. Drama plus, plus. I kept cool.

'Hi,' I said, the way you do.

We shook hands rather formally. Then Pamela dragged Brenda into the kitchen and we three sat in embarrassed silence pretending not to be aware of the raised voices in the background. I counted my fingers unnecessarily. Then turned to Terry.

'Good film?'

'Yeah, I thought so,' he said. 'Pamela didn't like it much though.'

This immediately struck me as a bit 'salt in the woundish'.

'Pamela's seen it?' asked Cloughie.

Terry looked a bit puzzled, and I puzzled why he was puzzled.

'Yes,' he said. 'With me.'

Cloughie's face indicated that the situation was not as advanced as I had surmised.

'With you! When?'

'Tonight,' said Terry and glanced at me. I nodded. Well, I knew that that had been the intention, though frankly I didn't really want to be drawn in.

'You're mad,' said Cloughie. 'She's been here with me.'

Terry told Cloughie that it was he who was mad and the argument was proceeding at playground level when Cloughie called to Pamela in the kitchen.

The girls returned and before any explanations could be demanded Brenda clapped her hands and called for quiet. Why? Because I'd just brought her a present and she wanted everyone to see it. She went through to the hall and they all stared at me. For some reason I felt guilty. I shrugged.

'It's not a geranium,' I said. Which didn't seem to help matters. More stares so I stood up and inspected a small ornament on the sideboard. Brenda came back wearing the helmet.

'Like it?' she said.

'You'll bloody need it,' said Pamela.

'Who is that?' said Terry. And everybody stared at him. I mean it was a full-face helmet but it was obviously Brenda wearing it.

82

Then she grabbed my arm and said: 'Come on, let's christen it,' and pulled me towards the door. I glanced back to see Terry take a pace towards Pam and say: 'You're Pamela.'

'And you're a pillock,' came the reply and then apparently she pushed him backwards over the settee. Actually I only heard of this petty violence the following day as by this time we were half way down the stairs.

It was rather late but Brenda said that a helmet could not be considered christened until you had travelled at least forty miles wearing it. We stopped at a club she knew in Southport and she had a vodka and lime and I had an extremely overpriced lager shandy. Then I got the whole story; at least I think so. You can never be completely sure with her, but it did fit in with the bits I already knew. It was very funny, especially the way she told it. She does have a very clever way with words and I've often thought that if she had put her mind to it she could probably have got English 'O' level.

By the time we got back the flat was in complete darkness. It was past two and I was feeling pretty shattered.

We stood by her front door and, well, I couldn't stay long. I had to go to work the next day. Or rather that day. I put my arms round her and she looked up at me, and we sort of moved our faces together. But the helmets clashed so we took them off.

That was our fourth meeting and though in comparison with the others it was rather short I did feel it could be described as a success. In fact as I drove home I felt very happy.

At the tunnel exit I noticed a patrol man staring at me, and I realised I was singing.

CHAPTER TWENTY-FIVE

She gave me till the next Wednesday. She said even that was generous and only because she was my sister. She had warned me time and time again but I took no notice and why should she put up with it and there were plenty of others who'd be happy to share and they'd pay their way which is more than I ever did and on and on.

So that was it. I had five days to find somewhere. Must say it took the edge off things. The best scam in the history of me, and what do I finish up with? The big heave. Top of the mountain to bottom of the well, in one. Shame.

I thought back to the previous night and the run to Southport. It had been one of those cool, clear nights you get after a hot day, and as we drove back along the Formby bypass you could see more stars than you ever knew were there. Malcolm stopped at one point, but it was only to tell me which one was a planet and how you could tell. Funny isn't it, how people who know everything know nothing.

Back at the flat he 'saw me to the door', as they say. It was a bit awkward; well, I've never been much taken with that business. Pam has always done enough for both of us. But it was OK. Nice even. Then he'd said, 'See you tomorrow?' and I'd said, 'OK,' and he'd said, 'Great.' And so it was, Grapes at six again. We were both on time.

I didn't mention my little problem. Just let him gab a bit. He told me, with a touch of smirk, that Terry had been dead narked about being taken for the berk he was the day before. I guessed the poser had given Malcolm a hard time now and again. Then he told me his mother had a cold and a few other dead interesting things like that. I nodded regularly but he must have spotted that I was on auto-pilot and he pushed me into telling him what was up.

He seemed genuinely sympathetic although not as surprised as he ought.

'What about your mum's?' he asked.

I told him it was too noisy for me, and I was explaining how my Mum and our Sandra and my Nan are always arguing, when he said: 'Don't you get on with your Mum?'

Maybe he was cannier than I'd credited or maybe I wasn't playing well, being a bit on the devastated side, but there seemed no point in defending her anymore. So I explained how, with a family of four, my mother had three favourites and I was none of them. Truth was that the noise I couldn't take was that of her crowing. She'd said I would be back inside three months because our Pamela wouldn't put up with me. If I'd gone back then she'd have been right with a month to spare. I then told him how she'd never understood me and reckoned I was a messer and that I told lies and that I was always causing trouble. I watched his face very closely but he managed to stay looking very neutral.

'Have you no other friends?'

'Of course,' I said. 'Loads.'

'Could you not move in with any of them?'

I explained how it wasn't that simple and that I was out of touch and that most of them still lived at home and those that had flats were paired off and that it never works with three. He said there were three girls in the flat below Pam's, so I pointed out that they were students and didn't count. Then we sat quiet for a bit.

That was new. I'd not met anybody who could just sit and not talk. Usually we all chat because if you don't people feel something's up, but it didn't seem to bother Malcolm. I wondered to B2 why it had taken all that time for me to notice this side of him. She said it was probably because I never shut up; so I sent her home. That day everyone was against me.

We sat quiet a bit longer.

'Why is it?' I thought.

'What?' Malcolm said, and I realised I'd been thinking with my mouth in gear.

'Why is it,' I said, 'that people don't understand when you're just kidding, just having a laugh?'

'Do you want me to be honest?' he said.

'No,' I said.

'Then I've no idea.'

'All right,' I allowed, 'but not too honest.'

'You *are* a messer.'

I told him I couldn't help it and he said: 'So you're a compulsive messer.'

I tried to explain how I just had this imagination and how it sometimes sort of took off and I had to do things to keep up with it. He didn't understand, and just suggested an imagination bypass operation. Very comical. So I sent him for more drinks while I sat and had a sulk.

I thought back to school and how I'd got labelled just because of one little incident. I'd been sent to get the register from the history teacher's desk and I just happened to notice an envelope in his bottom drawer when I accidently opened it in case our test results were there and available for adjustment to remove the prejudice factor. Inside the envelope was a video; the sort they keep on the top shelf of the hire shop, so all I did was a little swop with one on the geography teacher's desk. Not the boxes, just the video. I think hers was called, 'Background to the Common Market.' Anyway, the next day, while she was having a sly drag in the corridor, 4B were watching, 'Emmanuelle Has Fun In Tasmania.' It was quite a short film.

Nothing was said but after that, whenever there was trouble, I was the first to be taken in for questioning.

When Malcolm got back it was obvious that he'd been thinking too because the wrinkles in his forehead gave him the look of a screw-topped bottle of mixed gherkins. I told him this, but he just said: 'Brenda, why don't you make an effort? Just try and keep your tongue under control.'

I was about to say, 'That's what my last bloke said,' when he anticipated with: 'No smarty answers. No tricks. No messing. That's if you can?'

'Of course I can,' I miffed. 'I only do it to liven things up for people. I can be as dull and boring as the rest of you if I want.'

'Try it,' he said.

'If you're not careful I will,' I threatened.

'OK then.'

'Right.'

'From now.'

'Fine,' I said, 'though what good it will do anybody, God only knows.'

He then twittered on like a few other old women I've met; but I'd said I would be good, so I was.

And I was good the next day too.

When Pam got in from work the place looked like a Pledge commercial. The sideboard shone and the mirror sparkled and I'd even cleaned off those marks on the corner of the telly by the wastepaper basket where people had regularly got an in-off with an apple core. There were no tights drying over the sink, or furry fry pans congealing under it. I'd also got the unironed clothing tower down to half a metre. She hid her amazement with great skill and headed for the bathroom. In there I had rediscovered the window sill by dumping all the empties of shampoo, anti-perspirant, deodorant, hair conditioner, vanishing cream, shaving foam (Pam's legs), bubble bath, kaolin, hair spray and Flash (Pam's neck).

'I've bought new toothbrushes,' I called. 'Yours is the yellow one.'

'I don't like yellow,' she said.

Well, I knew it was going to be uphill.

Soon as she came back I gave her her dinner on a tray in front of a nicely warmed-up News North West. Then stood back respectfully. All that was missing was the black frock and frilly pinny.

'Good day?' I asked.

She ignored.

'Afraid it's mash spud,' I said. 'I was going to do

87

roasties but I pre-boiled them and they sort of disintegrated after half an hour.'

She just ate.

It was quite an original meal. I'd sliced some carrots, halved some sprouts and cut fish fingers into squares. Then fixed the lot on a couple of long skewers and twined spaghetti round. I called it fish finger kebabs.

'All right?' I asked.

She just looked, and took another bite. Then paused in mid-munch.

'Where did you get the skewers?'

'Top cupboard,' I said, 'standing in a jam jar.'

She yelled, spat out and upset the tray all in one go.

'That was turps,' she shouted.

I told her I'd wiped them first but she just ran past with her mouth open ready for the kitchen tap. Then I remembered.

'Pam,' I shouted, 'I've just washed the kitchen floor. It's still wet.'

Next day the students complained that the big bang from our place had caused an enormous crack in their ceiling.

CHAPTER TWENTY-SIX

He didn't care much for riding in the sidecar and cried all the way there and all the way back. However, the anti-Panleucopenia injection didn't bother him at all though that was probably thanks to the special skills of Mrs Scott. She's very good; warm and caring but firm and assured. I've often thought I might have been a vet, but I'm apprehensive with Rottweilers.

As I came in through the kitchen and gently put him in his basket I could hear mother talking on the living room phone. She called that it was for me and I said I'd be there in a minute once I'd washed my hands. As I did so I heard her say that she was feeling a lot better and that it had been just a bug. I was puzzled. You see, I can usually guess from her tone who she is talking to. With Mrs Lloyd Roberts and above, mother is very mid-Cheshire. With relations and friends she's Lancashire going on Widnes depending on their Rateable Value. Then for trades persons she shifts to atonal Merseyside, descending to pure Birkenhead if she doubts their competence. This one evidently triggered an odd mix near the Lloyd Roberts' register.

I took the phone and for a moment didn't realise who it was. Then it clicked.

'Brenda,' I said. 'Why the funny voice?'

She lapsed into normal as she told me it was part of the new image. I didn't see the relevance, but if she felt she should then why not. And she is very good at accents. I asked her how things were going and she told me how her efforts in the flat had gone largely unnoticed and unappreciated.

Now it had crossed my mind that the advent of the 'new improved' Brenda might have resulted in Pam changing her ultimatum. She did!

Apparently Brenda had created this highly original dish just for her sister and Pam's response was to change the deadline for Brenda's departure from Wednesday to Tuesday. When I hear how cruel siblings can be I'm glad I haven't got any.

We chatted on a while and I was glad to hear that Pam's unfairness had not weakened Brenda's resolve. She told me of a number of jokes she had resisted making and rejoinders she had left unsaid, but then had to ring off in a hurry when she heard Pam at the front door. She was also being good about phone bills. Her parting whisper sounded like, 'see you at tea' but I guessed I'd misheard and it must have been, 'see you at three'. Anyway, I knew I could clarify when I rang back later as she hadn't said where.

My mother had Beethoven on her knee consoling

him, which he accepted as his right without caring much what he was being consoled about.

'Well, that was a pleasant surprise,' she said.

It was certainly a surprise – Mrs Scott is quite deft with a needle – but how a vaccination against Feline Infectious Enteritis could be described as pleasant was beyond me. Then it dawned that she was talking about Brenda.

'Seemed very nice,' she went on. 'Asked if I was feeling better. Very solicitous. And very well spoken. Didn't sound at all Liverpool. Mind nor does Derek Nimmo, or Rex Harrison.'

I was thinking, 'Well, you're not exactly Glenda Jackson' when she took the wind out of my sails with the addendum: 'Anyway, I've asked her round this afternoon.'

Brenda said she regarded it as a challenge. If she could behave in the company of 'that toffee-nosed old trout' she would have really done well. Considering she had never met my mother and had only heard of her through me I thought her description quite uncalled for. I told her a genuinely reformed Brenda would not be so rude. She apologised and substituted middle-aged for old.

I was very apprehensive. As it turned out things did go well; at least to begin with. What I'd forgotten was that, although Brenda talks a lot, she's a Trappist Nun (if there is such a thing) compared with my maternal parent. Mother hardly stopped for breath throughout the first two rounds of Earl Grey and strawberry scones. Brenda just emitted the occasional slightly aspirated, 'Yes' or 'Amazing', and sipped like a second Lady Bracknell.

I must say she looked good. A tasteful red and white summer dress and a few kilos less make-up than she usually sports. I wondered why she didn't always look like that. But then this wasn't the real Brenda, was it. This was just her dressing up as, what she would call, 'a wooly back Wendy'. It was all a game. Still, she played it very well.

90

I was disturbed from my reverie by the instruction to, 'Show how it works.' They were both staring at me; then mother nodded towards the sideboard.

'The lighthouse,' she said. 'Oh he's a dozy Doreen.'

Brenda nodded her agreement with uncalled for vigour. I gathered that my mother's current rambling related to the Friends of Leasowe Lighthouse and her highly significant role therein. She was pointing to the model I had made.

'It was our totem,' she said.

I placed it on the coffee table.

'Well, go on,' she said. 'Flash it.'

Brenda spluttered. I pressed the switch on the base. It flashed.

My mother subsequently moved on to the subject of birdwatching and made a few disparaging remarks about my hobby: 'You'd not catch me getting up at the crack of dawn to go looking for the lesser-crested nut cruncher,' she said.

'Nuthatch,' I corrected, but she just ignored me and said to Brenda: 'I don't suppose you see many birds around your way?'

'Quite a few actually,' Brenda replied.

I added that she lived near Sefton Park which caused a raised eyebrow from across the table. I didn't mention that it was a two-room flat in an old Victorian pile.

'What are the rates like in that area?' my mother asked. Brenda, looking strangely innocent, replied in her best Sue Lawley: 'Oh we don't have any. But we think there may be mice in the cellar.'

Later, when my mother had taken the tea things through to the kitchen Brenda asked how I thought she was doing. I congratulated; then suggested we might move on but denied it was because I thought she was cracking. Then she said: 'Tomorrow's Sunday.'

I pondered what sarcasm that statement of the obvious would have triggered had I said it to her. Though perhaps not. Not from the new Brenda.

'What about somewhere special?' she went on. 'Something that really appeals to you. Forget me.'

'Aren't you coming,' I asked, mystified.

'Course I am, you . . .' she stopped. Then: 'Of course I am, Malcolm. But let it be your choice. And I've just got to behave.'

She was high on her current success.

Odd isn't it how, suddenly given a completely open brief, your mind goes blank. I mumbled a few possibilities – but she said: 'Don't tell me. Make it a surprise.' So I did.

CHAPTER TWENTY-SEVEN

Sefton Park is OK. If it was anywhere else people would say it was splendid or beautiful or super, but we don't talk like that. It's a couple of miles right round and full of trees and grass and a lake – you know the sort of stuff they put in parks. And there's an aviary and a big green house in the middle that you could play volley ball in, if it wasn't full of triffids and giant rhubarb. Yes it's OK. OK for an afternoon out I suppose – but not if you live just round the corner. I mean the Tower of London is great for a visit, but not if you're a Beefeater on your two weeks' annual.

Still, it was best behaviour time, so I didn't say anything. Just sat on the grass and chewed bits of it while he was up on the road close by, tinkering. Down by the lake a kid was offering some ducks the contents of his Mcdonalds' bag but they swam away. I didn't know ducks could read.

Dotted across the bank at indiscreet intervals were couples, some into heavy petting and some not so heavy, but none reading their library books. I wondered if this was what it was about. Was the Mackerel hoping to start off from where he had hardly started the other night? Was he hoping the proximity of these others, busy swopping tonsillitis under the cherry blossom, might inspire me, us? I'd read somewhere that they used to put china eggs in nests in case the hen needed reminding what to do. Maybe he'd read the same book.

He was still tinkering. Slack chain he'd said. Probably nerves. Anyway, it was a warm sunny day and I was trying to be good so I decided that even allowing for the fact that I hadn't really gone anywhere at all, he had, having come through from Meols, and it was his choice.

That's the trouble, you see. When you're a bit of a messer, a touch sarky now and again, then when you try and change, you swing too far the other way and become a saint.

And that day I needed to be.

I called up B2 and we mulled over those important things that you usually leave till too late like how far will I let him go assuming he tries to go further than I've decided to let him. And if he doesn't try that far do I encourage him or save the next bit for next time knowing that some of them want to start next time from where they stopped last time as if the first bit didn't matter. B2 was sure this didn't apply in Malcolm's case. So we mulled some more and chewed another grass stalk and wondered if he'd be dead corny when he came down and would start chewing from the other end like they did in this black and white movie we saw one afternoon last year that must have been older than my Nan and she remembers when you couldn't get bananas.

And he was still tinkering. So I decided, good resolutions or not, I'd have to have a little word. Well, it was spring and young girls have fancies to turn as well. I'd be gentle, discreet, just suggest that the view from half-way down the bank was worth a shifty. The kid had gone off looking for a litter bin prepared to accept his Mcdonalds, so maybe the ducks would come back. Malcolm could tell me what make they were.

Then he called to say it was fixed and we could move on. I should have known better. A month previous I'd thought a birdman was a biker and I was still being just as stupid. The reason he was up on the road tightening his chain was that it was slack. Now it was tight; so we moved. B2 reminded me that I shouldn't complain as I'd thought the park was too close to home and we were now leaving it. This was true. She then suggested that the Mackerel's game plan might still be as dishonourable as we had imagined and that he simply had in mind a more isolated pitch. Perhaps deeper grass and without the company of the formation wrestling team. Anyway, who needs china eggs?

We turned left into Lark Lane which B2 thought might be a sign. She's corny like that. And how far did we go? Well, it's hard to be accurate but, to the nearest 200 metres, we went about 200 metres.

Suppose I had asked for it. A surprise. My only condition had been no birdwatching, but when we stopped and I realised what I'd let myself in for I wished I hadn't been so choosy. I mean, museums are pretty boring places at the best of times but they're supposed to be, aren't they? You can only think, 'Isn't that amazing' just so many times. After the fifth glass case the sight of an actual fragment from the actual glass from Boadicea's actual shaving mirror leaves you thinking, 'so bloody what'. And this wasn't any museum. This was a motor museum.

Malcolm beamed our way in while I prayed some distant Scotty would beam me up. No such luck. We made our way down one side and he stopped in front of this pair of wheels joined by bits of an old hospital bed. As he knelt and prayed to it the bloke who owned the place appeared.

'Still in perfect running order,' he preened.

'Marvellous,' Malcolm marvelled.

'Knickers,' I thought.

The owner was a Malcolm clone plus wrinkles and they were soon talking bike Esperanto with him giving us the personal tour. Now, the only thing that's more boring than two blokes talking about new motor cars is two blokes talking about old motor cars. In this case it was old motor bikes, but just as lethal. I kept saying to myself, 'It's a test. He's chosen this lot on purpose.' And I did try. Believe me I tried. But there are limits.

Malcolm slavered over various piles of junk with names like the 1913 Mark Six Overhead Spam Tiger Intestine and the owner told us how he'd rescued it from some junk yard or bought it from an old lady for one pound fifty and a small tin of Whiskers. Then they talked about rallies for old bikes and Malcolm said he'd like to go to one and I think he was serious. He then told about his bike and the bit of chain trouble he was having and the bloke suggested something he might do and I still didn't suggest something they should both do. Then we came to the models.

Now Malcolm probably knows how engines work – he spends enough time playing with them – so it would have been easy enough to skip that bit. But no, it's lecture time, isn't it? And who's in the classroom? Just me. These models were like half an engine cut down the middle and when the fellow pressed a button the piston thing went up and down like – well, I didn't say it then and I won't now. I was behaving, remember. Malcolm stood back like the proud father who's missed the match one Saturday to take junior to the Grotto. And Santa droned on about compression strokes and crankshafts and I tried to keep my exhaust port closed (gob to you.)

'Of course,' he said, 'the trouble with a conventional engine is the piston has to change direction all the time.'

I believed.

'But if you look at this rotary engine you'll see a much smoother motion.'

I looked.

'This,' he said, 'is a Wankel.'

I won't bore you with the details but if there's one of you out there who'd have stayed good at that then I hope your halo strangles you.

95

CHAPTER TWENTY-EIGHT

Anywhere you like, she'd said. Well, I'd read about the Lark Lane Motor Museum but had never managed to get out that way. It was just brilliant. Bikes mainly, but a few cars and working models. I could have spent a week there. The owner, or should I say curator, came across when I was admiring a 1923 Norton. We got talking and I told him about my '39 Big Four and the Velocette I was restoring at home. It was instant rapport. Brenda and I were then privileged to a personal tour in which he took trouble to tell us far more than was on the display cards.

I suppose it was hard for Brenda, not having a mechanical background but he was very patient and gave a most succinct account of the four-stroke cycle using a half engine section as a visual aid. Then fantastico plus plus. Next to it was the only working model of a full-size rotary engine in the country. Perfect for illustrating the complex geometry of Dr Felix Wankel's masterpiece. But not to Brenda.

There was just no need for it. The owner would have been perfectly justified in demanding that we leave – without refunding one penny of the £1.50 entrance fee (75p each). I flashed an apologetic look. He took a deep breath, then carried on as if she hadn't spoken.

We discussed why the rotary engine had never really caught on. The problem seems to be an incomplete scavenge at low throttle. However, there is a new Norton Wankel which is a double rotary and it cuts off fuel to one chamber at low power so that the remaining chamber has to work harder giving a better scavenge. When I turned Brenda had gone.

For a moment my inclination was to go after her, but then I thought not. If she was in that sort of mood it was probably for the best. And she didn't live far away. Perhaps I'd phone later or maybe call by. I decided to stay just another hour or so; save the rest for another visit. At this point I realised I wasn't actually giving the owner my full attention but suddenly I heard the words, '1925 Hupmobile'. We had stopped in front of this huge American car. Beautiful it was. Deep blue with massive hemispherical head lamps and a glittering chrome radiator. He opened the rear door and ushered me in.

'She's available for hire,' he said, 'for that special occasion.'

From the dark of the back seat I heard: 'Not to you, buster.'

It was Brenda.

I climbed in as bid and sat beside her.

'I'll be back shortly,' he said, and closed the door. It was strangely quiet in there. I didn't tell her I'd thought she'd left and just said, 'Hi,' the way you do. She didn't answer so I inspected the interior. A hinged lid in front of us opened to reveal a compartment with a bottle of champagne and two glasses.

'Very chic,' I said.

Still no response, so I remarked on the spaciousness of the vehicle.

'Yes,' she said. 'Perhaps I could move in here. Nice furniture and there's probably a toilet in the glove compartment.'

There was something in her voice. A slight catch perhaps. Certainly a tone I'd never heard before. I realised that in my enthusiasm for the excitements of that afternoon I'd forgotten Brenda's accommodation problem. She blew her nose.

'You OK?' I asked.

'Fine,' she said and nodded to the bottle. 'The bubbles got up my nose.'

I wanted to console her but it was one of those times when there was nothing to say, but you still do, and it's usually fatuous.

'Something will turn up,' I said.

'Will it?' she replied.

I wracked my brain frantically trying to think of what might turn up. I so much wanted to say something positive. But you've got to be careful. Not too impulsive. On the other hand she only had two full days left. Really if it came to an emergency – well, there was only mum and me at home. I hesitated, then finally took the plunge. There are times in life when you've just got to be decisive and I'd decided that this was one of them. One of those times. I took a deep breath.

'Brenda,' I said, 'if by Tuesday Pamela hasn't relented and you're still determined not to go back to your Mum's and none of your friends are prepared to, well, able to help, then if you're really stuck . . .'

But the door opened and he was there clutching some pamphlets and a form with a large picture of the Hupmobile at the top.

'I got you these,' he said. 'In case you wanted it, for a wedding.'

There was a bump and Brenda stood up and hit her head on the roof. Then she was out the door.

CHAPTER TWENTY-NINE

I'm not the miserable type. I don't let the weather, the News at Ten or the phase of the moon upset me. Not like some. Life's too short and I've met too many who spend their lives on permanent winge. But for once things just got too much. I'd moved away as the twin bores Wankeled on and I found this first cousin to a hearse parked in a corner. Settled in the quiet of the back seat I did a bit of stock-taking. OK, so the reformed Brenda had blown it, but she'd been pushed way beyond the limits of human endurance. First, I'd been looking forward to an afternoon out and we hadn't gone far enough to change the post code. Then on England's only hot and sunny day of this century we were stuck in the sort of place you'd only bother with if you were caught down Lark Lane in a hurricane and you'd just had your hair done. And all of this on top of being a homeless waif who hadn't even got her own cardboard box to doss in.

Mind, it was the last one that was the real problem. The others would fade but the prospect of Tuesday, and me Charlie Chapling down the road to nowhere was dead depressing. And I got to thinking why and I knew I couldn't really blame Pam or the Mackerel. It was me, and I couldn't change. Yes, dead depressing, but I didn't mean it to show. So when he joined me in the back of the car and got all sympathetic I really wanted out. The crunch came when the boss man arrived back and triggered my ejector seat with that terrible word that begins with 'w' and ends in 'ding'. Next I was outside with a sore head and Malcolm steering me to the balcony caff for coffee and an aspirin.

I needed time to think so I suggested he went back and finished his tour of the scrap yard. Then I called up B2 and got to discussing the situation logically and systematically the way they say our lot never do. After two more cups things were falling into place. Maybe I needed that bump on the scone to put some sense into it.

B2 didn't take much convincing. With prospects down to zilch in the home town it was obvious that the thing to do was play away.

Then Malcolm came back. I assumed we were going but he delayed, saying that his new friend had gone to get something to show him. Something very special. Very historical. I guessed it might be Fred Flintstone's jockstrap. We waited.

'Let's go for a drink,' I suggested. 'I've something to tell you.'

'OK,' he said. 'Soon as he gets back.'

He arrived with this strip of white material which wasn't Fred's J.S.

'What do you reckon?' he asked.

Malcolm didn't know either. The bloke held it out and we both stroked it as if a bit of kindness might persuade it to confess. The suspense was yawn making.

'This,' he said solemnly, 'is the scarf Geoff Duke wore when he won the double in the Isle of Man TT in 1951.'

'Wow,' I said, 'and I thought it was a winter wooly for your Wankel.'

And it wasn't even funny.

CHAPTER THIRTY

She hadn't changed. It was crazy to think she ever might have, could have. So we left. I told the owner I'd be back again soon and he expressed the hope that I would, although there was an unspoken, 'on your own I hope' behind his smile. I didn't feel as annoyed with Brenda as I might. Her silly remarks had seemed lame, almost sad.

It was as if I'd caught a glimpse of another side of her but one that she didn't want anyone to know about. I began to see the repartee as some sort of protection. Without it she was vulnerable, exposed even, and although she'd played the game of 'behaving' as she called it, it had always been just a game. Like someone who gives up smoking for three hours to show that it's not a habit. She needed her smart answers to sustain the image. Without them she was a tortoise without a shell. A beetle on its back. A butterfly trapped in the secondary glazing. Yes, I'd got the metaphors. What I couldn't get was the 'why'. And what was she hiding?

I drove to the Britannia and we sat outside and looked out across the river. In the distance we could see the Clwyd range and I was about to point out Moel Famau when I remembered she'd said she had something to tell me. Before I could ask, she announced: 'I'm going.'

I forgot about Moel Famau.

'I feel so much better now,' she went on. 'It's making

100

up your mind, isn't it? Once you've reached a decision it's like as if a weight's been lifted off you. Like when you've bevvied too long and have got the wirlies. You stagger home feeling lost, stick your head down the big white telephone and shout for Hughie, and you're great again.'

I felt confused. In part due to the euphemistic nature of her parable but mainly I wanted to ask, where? why? when? Yet all I could say was: 'Who is Hughie?'

She demonstrated by exhaling the name in tandem with an elaborate retching performance.

'Mind, you never do that sort of thing, do you, Malcolm?' she said. 'Never go out and just get legless.'

It was true that I had never understood the attraction of excessive drinking. There had been one occasion many years ago – Tony's stag night it was – when I had been, not to put too fine a point on it, sozzled; but I think someone slipped something into my cider. Anyway, I felt so bad the next day that it taught me a lesson and I've kept things well under control ever since. I didn't tell her any of this and she went on:

'Mind, I don't these days. Used to when I was younger – when I was a teenager.'

'Like last year,' I countered.

'Watch it, Grandad,' she said. 'Life isn't numbers. It's what you've done and where you've been. And that's the answer. I'm going to start living again. I'm going to London.'

'London!' I echoed.

'Of course,' she said. 'Where else is there?'

She spoke as if it was axiomatic but I could tell it was sheer whimsy. What is it with women that renders them incapable of looking at a situation logically and systematically before reaching a decision?

'Just because Pamela's throwing you out?' I said.

'No,' she said. 'I'm ready for a change. I love London. It ticks at my speed.'

I didn't even know she'd been there, but there was a lot I didn't know about Brenda then – and now I suppose. She said she'd been there 'loads of times' and accommodation was no problem.

'I've mates down there and I can always find a floor some place. It's a couple of years since but I'll find them. They may have changed their doss but they won't have changed pubs.'

She went on to tell me something of her exploits in the capital. It was another world. Her facility with accents was much in evidence. She talked of being Bridget the ex-nun who had given up the habit, and the drinks she got from blokes who wanted to teach her new ones. I heard myself say: 'If it's just free drinks you're after you don't do so bad here.' But the irony was wasted and she prattled on, and on. Stories of parties and pranks, booze and blokes, and always some mug taken for a ride, some poser deflated, some yuppie left with egg on his face. I wondered if it could all be true. And I saw the sparkle in her eyes and guessed it probably was. She summed up with: 'The thing about London is, it never signs off. Like every night is Saturday night.'

There wasn't much to say. Not for the first time I realised that my feelings about a relationship were at odds with those of the other party.

'How long for?' I asked.

'Don't know,' she said. 'Before it's been just a few weeks at a time. Then I've needed to come home for a rest. But I'm older now; more stamina. Perhaps this time, for keeps.'

She paused and smiled in wistful anticipation of excitements to come. Then she looked at me.

'I'll give you a ring when I get there.'

CHAPTER THIRTY-ONE

Back at the flat Pam was curled up in front of the box Sidneyless. I guessed they'd had a row but didn't ask as we still weren't speaking more than the minimals. Later when we were, she told me that he'd been going on about his home-made wine and his bark rubbings and it had all got on her nerves so she'd sent him back to Frodsham with some rude advice as to what to do with his new corking device.

I went through to the bedroom and checked my piggy sock. There was enough for a saver and still a bit to see me right for a day or so. I'd had a job at a pizza parlour one time and thought I might try that again. Then I remembered how I came to leave and realised it would have to be a different parlour. A different chain even.

Pamela came and stood in the doorway.

'Could we talk?' she said.

'To each other?' I asked.

'Yes,' she said.

I was keen that we should split still friends so I said: 'Look I'm sorry for what's happened and you're dead right. I am a pain but it's no good me trying not to be because I just cock things up and people get narked and I get miserable so I've decided.'

She tried to interrupt but I pressed on. 'I'm going to London. Tonight. If I get the midnight I'll have all of tomorrow to look for somewhere.'

Again she tried to speak but I was determined to say my piece.

'I know you said Tuesday but I'm sure you've got somebody else lined up and they might be glad to start a fresh week here. Like I said, I'm dead sorry and all that, and I hope we're still mates, and it's all probably for the best. Anyway, once you've made up your mind there's no point in hanging around, is there?'

She agreed there wasn't.

So that was that. I got my duffel and threw in my

other jeans, a couple of tops and all the clean knickers I could find. Then thanked Pam for putting up with me, promised I'd never call her Giant Haystacks again, and left.

I got to Lime Street with half an hour to spare, put my bag on the seat next to me and glared at anyone who came near. Normally it's a two and a half hour run to London but the Sunday midnight takes its time and doesn't get in till near six so there's chance of a decent kip. That's if you've space to, and if you can. Normally with me it's no problem – I can sleep on a clothes line if needs must, but for some reason that night I couldn't. I thought about Pam and how, after we'd had our chat, she'd been dead friendly and made a coffee and insisted on giving me a few extra quid which I didn't really want though I did need and in the end took provided it was a loan. She'd almost said sorry for giving me the big heave. I remembered that she'd started by suggesting we talk. Then I'd rabbited on and I realised she'd never got to saying what she'd wanted to talk about. Could be she decided to pull the deadline back to Monday and my news had meant she didn't have to say it. But no, I knew it wasn't that. In fact if anything she'd had the face of someone who was wanting to be friends again. Anyway, we were.

The midnight doesn't stop at Runcorn but goes straight through to Crewe. As it chattered over the bridge I looked downriver; the lights of the city gave the sky a sickly yellow glow. I thought of the Mackerel. He'd be flakers. Cosy in his winceyette. I bet B2 that he had a teddy. At least people in London didn't have teddies. Well, not the zany gang I know – knew.

As we rattled off into the Cheshire dark I found that if you put your face tight against the window and shaded your eyes you could make out lots of stars. I pointed this out to B2 but she was asleep. If he'd have been there he'd have stopped the train and given a talk on which ones were planets. Yes, he's certainly a one-off. From all he'd told me I realised that he must have always been a bit of a loner; the type who gets taken advantage of. Funny how when somebody tells you a story or describes something that happened to them, if you listen carefully, you can pick up far more than what they tell you. Far more than they even know themselves. His mate Leonard for a start. Obviously a right fly boy. I remembered Malcolm saying how they'd got friendly, 'just after I got my first bike'. That spoke volumes.

I curled up with my head on my bag. A dozing prat on the seat across the aisle had his Sony banging out in that tinny way they do, so I reached across and unplugged his headphone lead. He opened his eyes and looked at me. I stared back with a look that said next time I'll use scissors. He seemed to understand.

Malcolm's mother took advantage of him too. And Terry.

It wasn't right.

CHAPTER THIRTY-TWO

Colin Weston gave a short summary of tomorrow's weather from the corner of the living room, then reminded me to switch off before smiling his friendly good night. I said good night to him the way you do when you are on your own. You don't get that these days with the thing going on all night. Then I not only switched off but unplugged at the wall. It's safest. I checked that the french windows were locked and the back door bolted before getting my glass of milk and going to bed.

It had been a long day. One of those days crammed full of events that happen around you, which matter to you but you can't influence. Being a determinist this comes as no surprise, but it can still leave you depressed.

I don't get to sleep easily at the best of times and that night it was quite a while before old Morpheus caught up with me. So much to look back on. So little to look forward to. I wondered when she'd decided. In the park? Or sitting in the Hupmobile? Or in the café? And what was the trigger, or conversely the final straw?

And what a way to tell somebody. I mean, although one accepts that events on the grand scale are predestined there is a degree of flexibility at the individual level and this allows the normal courtesies to be observed. Consideration for another's feelings is really so fundamental. And anyway, what was so special about London? Perhaps our underground wasn't as extensive as theirs but one of our cathedrals was bigger. Than their cathedral, not their underground. And if you added together the number of times our three had won the league championship compared with the total for their nine – though, admitted, Tranmere's contribution wasn't that significant, and I supposed I'd better go back to supporting them with not much else to do on a Saturday; not that I'd gone very often before. In fact, it must have been three years, and I felt very drowsy.

I woke next day to the ringing of the phone downstairs and with the feeling that I'd only just closed my eyes. I thought I must have overslept and that it was Ambrose calling to find out where I was. Then I realised it couldn't be because it was still dark. What's more it was Monday and he was off.

It was Brenda.

She'd said she'd ring when she got there, but this was ridiculous. And I told her so. I mean, she hadn't considered my feelings when she'd decided to go, and now she was calling in the early hours for no good reason. She let me fume for a minute or two then said, 'Sorry' in a plaintive way. I told her it was no time to be calling anybody and my mother wasn't even up and

106

I looked at the quartz carriage clock on the sideboard to see what 'no time' was. The clock had stopped at ten past one which seemed strange as I'd fitted a new Ever Ready Gold Seal LR6 only two months prior. Then it dawned. Not outside – that was still five hours away. It dawned on me. The reason the clock said ten past one was that it was ten past one.

'Where are you?' I shouted.

'Shush, you'll wake your mother,' she said.

'Where are you?' I whispered loudly.

'Crewe,' she said.

'What's happened?' I asked. 'An accident?'

'No,' she said. 'I did it on purpose.'

'What?'

'Got off.'

'What?'

'The train,' she said. 'You're being very repetitive.'

'Why?'

'That's better. I've changed my mind. I'm not going to London.'

'Why tell me?'

She said I was shouting again, and that she had had a good think and she reckoned Pam had been warming round and would let her stay. I reminded her what time it was and she said: 'I know. Will you pick me up?'

'From Crewe!'

'It's still Cheshire,' she said.

Can you think of anything more inconsiderate? So I really let her have it; gave it to her straight. Told her she'd just have to wait until the next Liverpool bound train came in. She said that was hours away and she was freezing cold and if she died of pneumonia then I'd be sorry.

I didn't think I would be.

'Look,' I said, 'it's turned one in the morning. I've work tomorrow. It would be a ninety mile round trip for me to pick you up, run you home, then come back here.'

Then she did the rottenest thing of all.

107

'Malcolm,' she said, 'the real reason I don't want to go to London is because it means—' and she paused for effect' – leaving you.'

And I knew her, and I didn't believe her, and I was tired of being used, conned, taken advantage of. So I really told her her fortune.

At least I started to but her ten pence was running out.

CHAPTER THIRTY-THREE

As station waiting rooms go I suppose the one at Crewe is as good as any. It's warm, the benches are padded, and the timetable posters make good bed time reading. So I managed an hour's kip before he arrived, flapping his gauntlets and trying to look annoyed. A younger, less sophisticated Brenda would have said, 'What kept you?' but I just put on my eternally grateful face and showed my appreciation in the usual manner, as they say. Seems a couple of days of behaving had left their mark.

He ranted on for a bit about people who make snap decisions without thinking things through properly and then get themselves into difficulties and expect other people who are more careful and more responsible and don't ever act rashly to help them out, and I just kept nibbling away at his left ear lobe and saying sorry until the tape ran out. Then I gently reminded him that I couldn't help it because, as he was always telling me, everything is already mapped out anyway. I didn't really want to go to London but fate made me think I did so that he could collect me from Crewe at half two in the morning. He thought about this for a bit. Then got his own back by telling me that as I hadn't got a helmet fate said I'd have to ride in a freezing cold sidecar.

This, I'd forgotten.

My jeans were thin with vented knees so I took my other, newer ones from my bag and changed. He blushed and turned his head, and watched in the waiting room mirror. I put my other top on top of my first top and then a woolly on top of that; then I put on his scarf and my anorak, and I knew I'd still be frozen. He let me bleat about this all the way to the bike, then opened the sidecar and took out the big blanket he'd brought for me.

Swine.

I snuggled down wrapped tight and warm, and as I dozed into the journey home I wondered why he'd let me change. Eventually I gave him the benefit of the doubt and decided it was just his little revenge.

Fortunately I hadn't given back my key. I told Malcolm this proved that I was never destined to go in the first place; truth was I forgot. Either way I was able to sneak in without disturbing Pam from her much needed beauty sleep. Before I went to bed I wrote her a second note saying how much I'd matured since Friday and wondering if we could start afresh, and I tore up my first note which said: 'I've decided to give you another chance.'

That afternoon I woke bright and early with the feeling that I'd never been away, which I hadn't really. There was a note from Pam saying, 'Welcome home and don't forget the launderette.'

I tidied round a bit, peeled and chipped some spuds and got out a couple of cod fillets to defrost. I then spent half an hour making rude words with the alphabet spaghetti which upset my timing so that I had to rush round making the meal in time for her coming in which is why I forgot to go to the launderette, your worship. Then she was late.

In my eagerness to please the previous week I had washed the curtains and due to an over-long visit to the spin drier they fell well short of the fruit bowl let alone the window sill. With time to kill I decided the clever thing to do was to lower the curtain rail six inches and did. When Pam came in she said: 'That's clever.'

'Like it?' I asked.

'Ludicrous,' she said, and I knew things were OK again.

We ate. She asked how London was and I told her it was closed. Then filled her in on my adventures from Lark Lane to Crewe and back in my own hilarious style. She smiled once.

B2 gave me a nudge and telepathed that things might now be OK for me but Pam was a bit semi-detached. I wondered. Then guessed: 'Cloughie?' I said.

She nodded.

'Been cracking the whip, has he?'

'I could crack his head,' she said. 'He's just a spoilt kid who wants to have his cake and eat it.'

'I'd never thought of you as a piece of cake,' I said.

'He's gone all prissy since we had that nark last night. Still wants to see me though, "But you will make sure you put those personal letters I sent you in the paper shredder." Not the only thing of his I'll put in the shredder.'

I winced on his behalf. She went on imitating: ' "And have you not sent out those claims summaries yet?" He forgets that after a bank holiday everybody's got a bit behind.'

I consoled and resisting the observation that she had more behind than most, I just said: 'You're too good for him.'

'True,' she said, and fortunately wasn't listening too carefully when I added: 'He doesn't appreciate a good thing when he's having it.'

Yes all right, you think it's all too much. But it's very hard, you know. Me saying these things is a bit like you being hit just under the kneecap with a small hammer. You kick. I spout.

Still, I'm working at it.

CHAPTER THIRTY-FOUR

I don't remember the Monday. I know there was one and that fortunately Ambrose wasn't in. Terry told me that I zombied through most of it and on two occasions he'd found me comatosed in the stock room. However, I did at least have the sense to go in on the train that day. Had I used the bike I would have been the ultimate traffic hazard. It must be that if one is basically a responsible type, one instinctively behaves in a responsible manner, even when the upper levels of consciousness cease to function.

So I got through Monday. Terry coped. There are certain advantages in working for a firm which is sufficiently out of date to deter nearly all customer interest.

At home that evening I was quizzed. In fact, interrogated is probably nearer the mark, but again memory fails when I try to recollect the explanation I proffered. Fortunately our paths cross for only the shortest section of Monday evenings as she has Local History Soc. at seven. By the time she got back I was taking the earliest night I'd had since I caught the nasty 'flu bug that was going the rounds in November '87. (I got it on the 23rd.)

The subsequent breakfast wasn't easy. It began with a period of icy silence which was eventually given over to a solemn requiem for the decline of moral standards and finished on the matter of ultimate desolation, viz. 'What would Mrs Riley think of me coming in at 4.30 am?'

It is hard to convey to anyone who doesn't know my mother, or some similar mother, how ominous such a statement can sound. In truth our next door neighbour probably didn't even wake, or if she did thought nothing of it, or if she did think something of it, so what? But such rationale cuts no custard in the smouldering intensity of a Meols breakfast area. Suffice to say that night time is bad time, and persons

111

abroad after midnight during the week (slightly later at weekends) are either burglars or kerb crawlers or promiscuous baggage, the first being the least despicable. But, you say, this is Britain in the eighties. Surely such attitudes have passed on long since. Sadly no, and nor will they. They may be ridiculed by the young but they inexorably regenerate in the bosoms of the middle-aged. To varying degrees, of course. Believe me; I have studied this subject.

From my vantage of some thirty years, I can look to my juniors and see free thinking liberals, and to my seniors and see staid reactionaries, and in my contemporaries the beginnings of the transition. So why the change? Well, from my careful observation it would appear that the dividing line, or perhaps watershed would be more accurate, is marriage. What is it about that institution that stifles tolerance and social conscience and cultures the seeds of mistrust and blinkered self interest? Put another way, as Brenda once did, 'Why are married people such dickheads?'

Yet knowing all of this there remains the paradox that only my determinism can explain; I hope one day to get married – or something similar.

To return to the matter of my mother's disfavour, suffice to say that the good impression Brenda had engineered at their first meeting was never to be rekindled. She was patently a 'bad influence' and will doubtless retain that label until such times as mother decides to let me be an orphan.

That evening I sat in The Grapes with the bad influence and her sister as they discussed at length life's injustices, and in particular the sins of one Sidney Clough. Brenda was particularly vitriolic and expounded on how he took advantage of his helpmate and her naturally kind, warm, generous and loving nature. Pam didn't argue and I knew better than to raise even a questioning eyelash.

Brenda then described for my benefit what a superb secretary Pamela was and how her quiet competence and cool efficiency were not appreciated. I watched her closely as she told Pamela emphatically how she was a fool to herself for putting up with it, and I saw no sign of that second edge that such compliments would normally carry. Not, that is, until she prompted me to corroborate, and I tentatively joined in the spirit of approbation and said: 'Right, once they'd made Pamela they broke the mould.'

'You're not wrong, Malcolm,' Brenda said; then leaning across to remove an imaginary hair from my jacket whispered: 'And with the pieces were able to make three new ones.'

No, try as she might she could not desist from the one-liners. The only improvement was that at least the victim didn't hear.

I suggested some People Watching feeling instinctively that if Brenda continued to go OTT on Pamela's abilities she'd ultimately blow it with something more audible. So they played their strange game a while, with Brenda claiming to have checked out Pam's assessment of a character they called Mary who turned up in the launderette that day and 'cadged a ride for seven lisle stockings and a bird cage cover'. When we queried the odd number of stockings Brenda said one was for straining the chip fat.

I declined an invitation to play as with the pair of them at it I felt very fourth division, besides which I was feeling a residual jet lag even though I had had one full night's sleep. I explained saying I was still a little dopey and Brenda said that was true.

'If you will spend your nights kidnapping innocent young girls from cosy railway stations then it serves you right.'

I said I didn't know why I bothered for all the thanks I got, so she said: 'Thanks,' and I said: 'It's all right,' and Pamela said if we were going to have a row she was going home, and went.

Things *had* changed since Brenda's short spell of being good. But not much.

With Pam gone Pam became the subject of conversation. It's the way, isn't it.

But nothing nasty. In fact, Brenda was genuinely concerned about her mistreatment at the hands of Sidney Clough and indignant about his attitude to her.

'He's got it made,' she said. 'A plastic wife and labrador back home in Frodsham and his own personal snogographer here in town.'

She then went on, yet again, about how good Pamela was at her job adding: 'Like lots of secretaries she spends most of her time covering up his cock-ups for a tenth of his money.'

This struck me as a bit unfair. A factor of one quarter or a third was probably nearer the mark.

I asked how long Pam had worked at the Bootle and Bournemouth and Brenda said she'd gone there on leaving school. She told how Pam had started in the mail room and by virtue of her reliability and diligence, coupled with shorthand and typing skills acquired at evening classes, had progressed rapidly until she reached the plateau of personal secretary.

'Must have been there nearly ten years,' she said. Then stopped and thought. 'So don't you think there should be a party?'

'Why not?' I said.

'You're right, Malcolm. Why not?' she echoed. 'Next Friday you think? OK. At our place? Right. We could get some of her wrinkly mates along – she'd like that. We wouldn't want to stay though, would we.'

'Wouldn't we?' I asked.

'No. They're a bit of a pain, her lot.'

Then she added with the intolerance of the convert: 'They all smoke too; hate people who smoke, don't you?'

'I don't hate them,' I said. 'I'd sooner they didn't for both our sakes, but I don't hate them.'

In fact, I don't hate anyone, apart from Hitler, and Renton my form teacher when I was in 2B who used to call me Mable Stonehead because he'd heard Carter say it who was the class thug and Renton liked to

114

keep sweet with him. Then I thought back and I said:
'Anyway, didn't you once tell me you used to smoke?'

'Yes,' she said, 'and heavy too. But I gave up when
I was twelve. Now about this surprise party you
suggested. What about the booze? If you fix that up
I'll organise the eats.'

'Hold on a minute,' I protested.

'Quite right, Malcolm,' she said, 'Cloughie can organise the booze. We'll fix up the eats between us.
How are your fairy cakes?'

I felt bemused.

'Gee, Malc,' she said, 'how do you do it? When the
time calls for some really crazy ideas, we can always
rely on you.'

CHAPTER THIRTY-FIVE

Once upon a time in a little office half-way up a tall
building in the middle of a big pool there dwelt a
Slimy Sidney, looked after by his maidenly minder,
Pretty Portly Pamela. One sunny morning at about
twenty past eleven the phone in the little office said,
'ring ring,' and pretty portly Pamela picked it up
and said: 'Hello,' because she was very good with
phones.

'Hello,' said a tiny Scottish voice. 'My name is Mrs
McDougal and I'd like to speak to Mr Clough about a
wee insurance claim.'

'Just a moment, please,' said P.P.P. and handed the
phone to S.S.

He said, 'Hello, Clough here,' because he could see
his reflection in the glass door of the office. He listened, then said, 'Well, strictly the Home Contents
Policy doesn't cover pets. But tell me, how did he
come to singe his trunk?'

He listened some more; then said: 'Until the brigade arrived. I see. Yes, well, I'll be here, but there's no need for you to bring Henry with you.'

Then S.S. gave the phone back to P.P.P. the way very important people do who aren't very good at putting handsets on cradles.

At this stage you might be wondering how I got to know the details of this fairy story and you might guess that Pamela told me. Well, she could have but she didn't.

Half an hour later, just after Pamela had left the building to go for her lunch Mrs McDougal appeared as if by magic outside the little office. She knocked on the door: 'Tap, tap.'

'Who is it?' said Sidney.

'Mrs McDougal,' she said, though really this was a fib.

'Come in,' said Sidney. 'Oh, it's you.'

'Hi, Sid,' she said in a de-Scottished voice.

'Was that you on the phone?'

'Yes,' she said, 'but don't worry. I've left Henry downstairs. Those lift doors are a bit quick and might catch his ears.'

Sidney stood up and said: 'You have no business in this building. I shall have strong words with your sister when she gets back.'

At this point our story loses its 'U' Certificate so if you are under four, a *Sunday Sport* reader, or otherwise of a nervous disposition please move on two pages.

'Sit down,' said Mrs McDougal.

Sidney protested that she had no right to speak to him like that because he was a very important executive, so she was forced to return him to his five castored swivel with a flat palm to the ribs. She then held his executive snow scene paperweight delicately over his head while she explained the situation.

'Firstly,' she said, 'I do have business in this building. With you in fact. Secondly, you won't mention

116

my visit to Pamela because if you do I shall be forced to conduct this interview at 17, Antirrhinum Close, Frodsham.'

Sidney looked quizzical and Mrs McDougal said: 'Telephone book.'

'What do you want?' he then muttered, sounding a bit like a club owner in a forties movie when the protection mob pay a visit.

'Just you to be nice,' said the mob.

Looking as if he'd much prefer to cough up the forty grand Sidney said: 'What are you talking about?'

So Mrs McDougal spelt it out: 'Sidney, you are a mean, inconsiderate, conceited, thoughtless, two-timing flea bag.'

He swallowed his protest when she shook the paper-weight, then she went on: 'Which, as you were about to point out, is none of my business, except that it is my sister that you are taking advantage of, and I don't like that. So I want you to change. Not a lot, or she won't recognise you. What is needed is a spontaneous show of your affection.'

Sidney was very indignant and said that he had given Pam some wine glasses only the previous Christmas.

Mrs McDougal corrected him saying that he had given Pamela twenty-four coupons, and told her which petrol station she could pick the glasses up at.

'Your next idea,' she went on, 'will involve putting those glasses to good use. You, Sidney, have decided to throw a surprise party for your favourite secretary's anniversary. Can we use the flat, you say. Yes, that'll be OK. And you want me to fix up the food? Certainly, Sidney. What about the booze? Oh, you want to do that. That's fine then. And, Sidney, if for some reason you should change your mind, I'm afraid Mrs McDougal will feel compelled to make a mysterious phone call to Antirrhinum Close. And if that doesn't work she'll send Henry up here to sit on you.'

But she didn't need to and arrangements were made for the surprise party and it was only a partial disaster and they all lived now and then occasionally happily ever after or at least to the end of the month.

CHAPTER THIRTY-SIX

I could remember how you got the two little wings which stick up out of the cream. You simply cut a conical piece from the top at the centre, then split it into two. But I couldn't remember how you made the cream. Terry was no help. In fact when I told him I'd agreed to make butterfly cakes he was convinced that I was having my leg pulled. What's more he was sure it was Brenda who was doing the tugging. I suppose his unfortunate encounter with her the previous week had left him a touch cynical. Carefully I explained that on this occasion nobody was being taken for a ride. It was simply that Brenda had been passing the B & B the other day and Sidney had spotted her, called her in, and asked if she'd help fix up a surprise party for Pam's anniversary.

'What anniversary?' Terry asked.

So I told him that on the Friday of that week, Pamela would have been with the firm exactly nine years, seven months, and two weeks. Terry looked a little puzzled – well, quite a lot puzzled actually – but I was able to explain to him, as Brenda had explained to me, that if we waited for the round decade anything might have happened. Pamela might have left for instance.

He remained sceptical and was in fact quite caustic about Brenda. I felt very defensive being aware of her recent effort to change and the residual effects of her limited success. He opined that the trouble with

Brenda was that although she liked to take other people for a ride with her elaborate jokes and scams she would be very hostile if one was ever worked on her. Her type really had no sense of humour, he said.

This seemed a most unfounded assessment and I insisted that Brenda *would* see the funny side of any chicanery of which she was the victim, provided it was clever, nobody was physically hurt, and there was no damage to public property. I must concede that this was surmise on my part, as I had not actually discussed the matter with her, but it seemed a reasonable point of view. Terry and I argued for some time until we eventually hit on a scheme that would settle the matter. Friday seemed as good a day as any. It was already planned to an extremely tight schedule so it was possible to say precisely where each of us would be at a specific part of the early evening.

I managed twenty-nine butterfly cakes from just two packets of the mix. My mother made a suitable butter cream and in addition two dozen vol-au-vents plus the same number of sausage rolls, half of which were vegetarian, and an apricot sponge cake. You might think this extremely charitable considering her expressed attitude to the younger Wilson, but the truth was that when asked, I had given only an abridged version of the buffet's purpose. Having heard the function was to commemorate a friend's ten years of service she had assumed, as I thought she might, that the friend was a Waring's employee and I had not dissuaded her of this opinion. Being a strong supporter of the work ethic in general and company loyalty in particular she had offered to help. This solved my cream-making problem and also led to her production of the additional savouries mentioned.

On the Friday I called round to the flat in my lunch hour and delivered the food stuffs. Brenda said Sidney had been in touch and would be bringing the liquid refreshments later. It would help if I would

pick up Pam from work and bring her home; the
longer this took the better as they needed time, to get
things ready and for folk to assemble. I regarded this
as something of a challenge. Now, I know that on
occasions it has been said that I have a propensity for
prevarication and ambivalence. Well, perhaps not in
those precise words. But it is unfair. An apparent
equivocalness is often simply the signature of a thinking man. So I took time out to formulate tactics for
the necessary journey extension. However, when I
began to give the detail to Brenda she said that
communication of the minutiae was not necessary
and a simple ETA would suffice. Well, perhaps again,
not in those precise words. So I told her when we
would arrive and then left. However, I did ensure we
synchronised watches.

At five I was waiting close to the B & B as the
building disgorged its working populace. It was gone
quarter past before she appeared which was I suppose further proof of her dedication. I approached and
expressed surprise at meeting her. I said I was on my
way to her place as I was going out that evening with
Brenda and asked if I could give her a lift. I must be a
natural actor because she didn't suspect a thing. Just
said, 'OK.'

CHAPTER THIRTY-SEVEN

I'd got in touch with her best friend Clarissa who'd
then got in touch with the rest of their gang. The idea
was that they'd assemble in The Grapes while me and
Sidney got things ready at the flat. Then I'd ring
through and they'd all roll up together just before
Pam was due to arrive. Then lights out, Pam opens
door, lights on, Surprise Surprise, 'God luv us, it's all

120

me mates.' Kiss, kiss. Isn't Sidney wonderful to do all this? And the rest we leave to your imagination – or their imagination, what there is of it.

But why have them go to The Grapes – why not straight to the flat? Simply because some of her lot are known to be closely related to the Sicillian locust and given too much waiting time could quite easily eat the place out.

I explained this to Sidney but his only concern was that none of them were from the B & B. Apparently he imagined that nobody there knew about his over-time with Pam – seemed unlikely to me – but I assured him the selected friends were all local dipsomaniacs who wouldn't know him if they fell over him, which they probably would do during the course of the evening.

I laid the side table with Malcolm's cookery class homework and fixed nine and a half candles on the sponge cake. Then I put out the saucers of crisps, nuts and twiglets that I had so skilfully removed from their packets. Lastly I placed four large sliced loaves and some cheese and stuff on the kitchen table, this being the ingredients of the butties that I hadn't got round to making. They could help themselves. Sidney brought up the booze which consisted of six cases of elderberry, three turnip and one rice. He said it would benefit from having a little time to settle. I had a feeling that it wouldn't be too long before it was brought up again. I recommended that we hid most of it in various cupboards and under the bed on the grounds that if they had to hunt for it, it would slow them down. He had also, being the mad impetuous deputy assistant undermanager brackets claims that he is, brought some streamers and a can of silly string left over from the B & B's last Christmas party.

Then it was time to ring The Grapes. Malcolm was due to arrive with Pamela in just ten minutes so with the gang only five minutes' walk away everything was going like quartz-work.

So I rang. And it was engaged. So I waited, then rang again, and it was still engaged. So Sidney rang because he is a very important executive, and it was still engaged.

'Right,' I said, 'plan two.'

'What?' he said.

'There isn't one,' I said.

'Stupid,' he said, and if I'd had the paperweight handy he'd have been in his own private snow scene.

'Pamela always has a reserve strategy,' he said.

'Right,' I said. 'When she gets here we'll see what she suggests.'

I rang again. Still engaged.

But there was a way. Obvious really. Sidney could nip round to The Grapes in his car.

'I don't know them,' he protested.

'Just go in and shout Clarissa,' I told him.

His next excuse was that his car was parked three streets away so that Pam wouldn't see it.

'Then run,' I shouted.

'You go,' he yelled.

'Antirrhinum Close,' I breathed.

And he went.

I rang The Grapes. Still engaged. I paced the ceiling. I thought of getting the three students in from downstairs to be short notice understudies in the Surprise Surprise chorus line.

I thought of ringing Cilla Black.

I looked out of the window.

I rang The Grapes. Clarissa answered.

'Hurry up,' I shouted. 'No, don't hurry up. Take your time.'

I had just heard the putter-putter-plunk of an antique motor bike. I rang off. Then dashed to the door and bolted it. I put all the goodies in the sideboard cupboard and in the kitchen cupboard and on top of the unit in the corner with a tea towel over them, and the front door rattled and the door bell kept ringing and I hid the streamers and the can of silly string. Then I went to the door and took the bolt off.

'You go first,' said Malcolm.

Pamela came in. She was not pleased going on livid.

'Why did you put the bolt on?' she yelled.

'Sorry,' I said, 'I was testing it.'

She brushed past me.

'Surprise, surprise,' said Malcolm behind her.

She flopped into the arm chair and opened up another crack in the students' ceiling.

Malcolm followed, looking surprised.

'Where are they?' he whispered.

'Shut up,' I explained. Then to Pam in my most sisterly: 'You OK?'

'No,' she said. 'I had the misfortune to meet this pillock as I came out of work.'

The pillock, who was standing behind her, grinned and gave a stage wink.

'I gave Pam a lift,' it said.

'Yes,' she agreed, 'but first we had a fifteen-minute walk to the multi-storey. And do you know which level he'd parked on?'

'No,' I admitted.

'Nor did he,' she said. 'We had to get out of the lift at every stupid floor to look for it. Then, he remembered.'

Malcolm smiled and said helpfully: 'We were in the wrong multi-storey.'

'We were in the wrong multi-storey,' she echoed. 'So then it was another half-mile walk, and then which level was it on?'

'Top,' said Malcolm.

'He likes going to the top, don't you, Malc?' I said. 'Likes whizzing down the ramps.'

'Not this time,' Pam said. 'It was rush hour and it took us twenty minutes to get out. The fumes were terrible. And that sidecar gets all steamed up.'

I sympathised and said I could just imagine how awful it must have been for her, sitting there, like an oven-ready turkey in a microwave. She wasn't too keen on my mental picture but pressed on: 'Then he holds up all the traffic while he studies his map.'

'He's always keen to find a new route,' I offered.

'In a car park?' she said. 'Then we went off on a magical mystery tour, out through the festival site and half way to the bloody airport.'

'It's a lovely run by the river,' he said.

I gave him my best 'let's leave it' frown and said to Pam:

'The sidecar does get a bit hot and sticky. Why don't you go and freshen up? Then Malcolm can take us down to The Grapes and buy you a compensating pint of gin and orange.'

She threw him a dagger or six, sniffed under her arm, pulled a face then stood up. En route to the bedroom she glanced in the kitchen.

'What's for tea?'

'What?' I panicked.

'Nothing cooking?' she said. I'd forgotten Pamela's second favourite pastime was eating.

'Ah well,' I stalled, 'Malcolm wants to buy us both a takeaway because it's his motor bike's birthday.'

'How old?' she said.

'Fifty,' he invented.

'King prawn foo yung with fried rice,' she said and went into the bedroom.

'Well done,' I told him.

'Suppose I'm just a natural,' he said. Then went to the front door, opened it, shouted, 'Won't be long,' closed it and tip-toed back in again.

We took our time. Moving about very quietly we restored the goodies to their places. I put the cake in the centre of the table and lit the nine and a half candles. Then the gang arrived, but no Sidney. They'd missed each other on the way. I had visions of him standing in the corner of The Grapes shouting Clarissa and all the regulars pretending not to notice.

We gave everybody a glass of Sidney's turnip and swore them to stillness around the room. I was about to check in the bedroom that she was OK and ready to be surprised when the door bell went. Everybody froze. I nipped through to the hall. It was Sidney. Quietly I closed the door behind him as I whispered him up to date. What I didn't know was that while I was out there Pamela called: 'Will you get that?'

And there was nothing anybody could say because they weren't there. When we came in Malcolm gave Sidney a drink and I stood him at the centre of the group.

'Brenda,' shouted an annoyed Pamela, 'Will you answer the flamin' door! Do you hear me? Brenda!' And she opened the bedroom door and came out and somebody threw a streamer and somebody else fired the silly string and everybody shouted, 'Surprise Surprise,' and Pamela yelled and ran back in again.

Malcolm said that he'd got a mole in a similar spot.

The Grapes was quiet. Peaceful even. You can't beat the relaxing atmosphere of a traditional British pub. I suppose it's the combination of flat beer, mucky glasses and dusty Christmas decorations still up in June.

I'd managed to talk Pamela round and convinced her that although it was all Sidney's fault his intentions were for the best, and she should forgive him. As we left she was forgiving him under the sideboard while the rest of them forgave each other in a variety of pairings all over the flat. Malcolm remarked on the rate they were putting away the home brew and I explained that that crowd would drink Liquid Ajax if someone else was buying. Sidney had confided in Malcolm that he had hidden away some of the elderberry to give it chance to mature. We reckoned they'd find it about half-nine so hoped it was matured by then.

Still, all things considered, it looked as if the party was a success. Sidney and Pam were friends again and the good will was flowing through the building. The students from downstairs had called to borrow some Polyfilla for their ceiling and had finished up in the bathroom drinking three-week-old rice wine and

Pepsi from a plant pot holder. Clarissa had clicked with old Mr Haygarth in the flat above and was last seen on the top landing inspecting his war wound.

But we were glad to be out of it. I congratulated Malcolm on the way he had delayed Pam's arrival; it had been well thought out and she had been completely fooled by his performance. Of course he does have the advantage of already looking stupid. He preened, then, flushed with success, suggested some People Watching. Seemed to think that all of a sudden he was ready for the big league.

'What about him?' he said.

There was a Newy by the door: a bearded bloke wearing dark glasses, jeans and a check shirt. Very possible I thought.

'I'll go first,' he said. And I enjoyed a smirk at his naïve confidence.

'Hungarian,' he said. 'No, better still, Canadian. Yes, that's it, a French Canadian lumberjack with a wooden leg.'

'Not bad,' I said.

Malcolm was a bit pleased with himself and pressed on with: 'Hobbies include playing the organ whilst balancing everyday objects on his nose.'

Better. He was beginning to get the hang of things and I told him so. Then just as I was about to devastate with a real expert's assessment the bloke limped across to the bar. Wooden leg. Malcolm must have seen him come in. OK, two can play at that game. I held fire while the bloke ordered a drink; then we heard Harold say: 'Sorry, mate. Don't change dollars here.'

'*Comment, Monsieur?*' he said.

'No dollars,' said Harold, whereupon the bloke stepped away from the bar, put his head back, rammed a match box on his nose, took a mouth organ from his pocket and started to play. Everybody stared, especially me. Harold remonstrated and shouted that he hadn't got a music licence. I turned on Malcolm.

'Who is that?'

'I told you,' he said. 'A French Canadian lumberjack with a wooden leg whose hobbies include playing the organ whilst balancing everyday objects on his nose.'

He took off his beard and came across. I just said: 'Bastards,' because that night the drinks were on me.

CHAPTER THIRTY-EIGHT

We were well cast. Terry was entirely convincing as the French Canadian lumberjack and his extrovert nature allowed him to enjoy the centre stage performance with matchbox and mouth organ. No way could I have coped with that, but my innate deliberative skills were ideally suited to the role of *agent provocateur*.

She took it well. Didn't actually laugh, but smiled. We told Terry the tale of Pam's surprise party and he laughed. Then I told a joke about a chap from Hemel Hempstead, a gorilla and a bucket, but nobody laughed because I got the ending wrong. But it was a good evening, and we had a few more like it. Not with Terry. Just Brenda and me. Pictures mainly, plus a couple of pop concerts and a disco on Saturdays. We even saw a play. I suppose it must have been about three weeks' worth of good times. For me it was quite a change. I'm more inclined to take my pleasures in cahoots with Mother Nature. Discos, in particular, I find noisy and stuffy places – but it's different if you're with somebody; somebody you like. And we did get on OK. Occasionally she'd say something or do something at which I could have taken umbrage, but it's not worth it, is it. Life's too short.

I've always thought there are too many umbrage-takers around. Folk who spend their lives taking offence over things said or done, by friends or relations. I'm sure you've met them. Sad, isn't it, when the only topic of conversation people can muster relates to the slights they've suffered. They should all be sentenced to a week with the old Brenda; that would cure them. Even the new model could deliver at least two buckets of umbrage fodder in a normal evening. But as I said, I just let it swill past me.

And we were happy. At least I was – and she seemed to be. Subsequently I was given to wonder if, for her, the whole interlude wasn't just a boring charade, but she seemed content enough at the time. Mind, I'm not the world's best at seeing through people. Tend to take them at face value. Bit naïve I suppose; and I don't learn from experience the way I should. After all, another word for determinist is fatalist and I should have remembered that the one guarantee in life, is death. The surest thing about happiness, is that it will end. As we transit the Cumbrian Fells of emotional experience the one certainty is, that on reaching a peak no matter which way you move off, you must go down (Stoneway 1959–). It may be a gentle slope, or a steep escarpment or even, as it was in this case, a precipice, but down you most definitely go.

There was a certain irony about the way events unfolded. Now, with the benefit of distance, I can look back on those first months of the Brenda saga and see a strange symmetry. To extend my mountaineering metaphor the two ends of the transit had a similar shape. Our first meeting was linked to a minor accident and subsequently a day's birdwatching. Similarly the precipice I've just mentioned came after a day's bird-watching and an accident, although this latter was certainly more serious than a spilt drink.

Leibnitz (1646–1716), being both a mathematician and a determinist, would have admired the elegant congruity. Stoneway didn't.

But I'm racing.

One evening, during those heady plateau days, I was at home engrossed with a repair to the lighthouse

model (necessitated by a duff trimmer capacitor; 20%
tolerance they claim – big joke), to the accompani-
ment of my mother's rambling account of that
afternoon's committee meeting. She can be extremely
long-winded about the most trivial of incidents and at
such times I feel inclined to offer a short prayer of
thanks that that particular character trait (pro-
nounced *tray* in some circles) is not hereditary.

She told how she had waited until Any Other Business before delivering the bombshell that she was not
prepared to run the tombola at the next summer fête.

'Well,' she said, 'you could have cut the silence with
a cake slice. I told them I'd had enough. Last year it
barely broke even at five corks for 20p and there they
were talking about making first prize a bottle of
whisky. They said they'd ask Ethel, but there's no
way she will. At the moment she's up to her eye
shadow with the costumes for Iolanthe and it's
putting years on her. I know, I've had some. I did
them for the Wallasey Chrysanthemums way back
and you can't trust the fairies. They all claim to be
two sizes smaller than they really are, and you're left
splicing in acres of taffeta right up to the dress
rehearsal. Which reminds me, I've booked four seats
for the Friday.'

I asked why four and she explained that Peggy and
Bernard were coming over.

'Bernard loves G and S,' she said. 'Sang with the
Bentley for years but his voice went a bit unpredictable after he had his prostate done. That's why he
left and joined that barbershop crowd.'

I had heard from another source that Bernard's
move was more to do with his wandering eye than
wandering pitch. Apparently after a well remembered
rehearsal for *Pirates* the lead soprano announced that
if a certain PC wasn't relieved of his truncheon they
could find another Mabel. Still, mother knew nothing
of that and was content with her own ill-informed
explanation.

'I told him he should have gone private,' she said.

'Some of those National Health surgeons wouldn't know a scalpel from a pair of pinking shears.'

I was about to hum a short chorus of 'Poor Wandering One' when she said: 'Would you be wanting another ticket? For a, *friend* perhaps?'

I didn't bite. Just said: 'Shouldn't think so.'

But she pressed on: 'No, nor should I. You don't have much in common, do you?'

'We get along OK,' I said. 'Gilbert and Sullivan isn't to everyone's taste.'

'It's not taste, it's culture,' she said. Then, after a pause: 'It won't work, you know.'

'Mother,' I said, 'we're just friends. Friends who occasionally go out together.'

'Three times last week. Mind, I bet it's always her choice. When did you last go birdwatching?'

'A few weeks ago now,' I said vaguely. It had been the weekend after the Chester fiasco which had left Brenda and me more than a bit incommunicado.

'Who with?' she asked.

'Leonard and James and Annette and some others.'

'Yes, well, you were wise not to take her. You'd have been so busy keeping your eye on her you'd not have had chance to look at any birds.'

'Mother,' I said, 'Brenda is not interested in birdwatching or motorbikes or watching Tranmere Rovers, and nor are you, come to that, so there's no point in trying to make a big issue of it. We still find plenty of things to do together.'

Well, perhaps I could have chosen my words better, but that's the difference between talking and writing, isn't it. Anyway, she gave a hard stare, so I went to make the supper. I filled two cups with cold milk, sprinkled the Ovaltine on top (you don't stir), and placed them in the microwave. As I keyed in three minutes fifty I wondered if Brenda could tolerate G and S. That would certainly be one in the eye for old snotty next door. A real Eliza at Ascot touch. But then I'm no Higgins – no wish to be. No, that wasn't what Brenda and I were about. Still, it did cross my mind that the sharing of some outdoor pursuit would give our relationship an extra strand.

And so it did, but I never imagined that it would be ornithology, or that she would initiate it, or that its pursuit would inexorably lead to the aforementioned precipice.

CHAPTER THIRTY-NINE

It was our Pamela's fault. If she hadn't goaded me, I wouldn't have defended him and his stupid game. Then I wouldn't have had to carry it through and go trekking off across a chunk of imitation Dartmoor to sit in his stupid Wendy House. Up to then things weren't so bad. I mean, he could be a boring old pillock if I let him but a swift elbow to the left gut worked wonders. Either that or a gentle little witticism, the type that some have been known to get a touch niggled about, but Malcolm accepted. Because they were well earned, I suppose.

We got around a bit too. Clubs, pictures, concerts. Saw The Christians at the Empire and Chris de Burgh at an open air do down by the river. Out of fairness I let Malcolm choose once (just once), and we saw a play called *Shirley Valentine*. Very funny and just like my Auntie Eileen, but that Everyman Theatre must be dead hard up as they could only afford a cast of one.

It was mostly weekends that we went out and somehow it made the rest of the week seem pretty boring. Don't misunderstand me, I wasn't missing him or any of that rubbish – just bored. So I was glad when Friday came round. He was working late, stock-taking or something, so we'd agreed to meet in The Grapes and then go on somewhere. Pam came with me as the Frodsham Ferret was due at the flat later with his latest parsnip and she felt she ought to have a drink first.

I suppose we got there too soon but it was either that or watch Paul Daniels. Anyway, we had a couple and got to talking about things like men, which included Sidney and Malcolm because they are a *bit* like men. She said it must be a record, me still going out with the same bloke after all that time, and I said I was just free-wheeling for a bit until something more interesting showed up. I told her she'd be better changing bikes more often and next time should go for something that wasn't already carrying a ferretess in the saddle bag. I pointed out that there was no future in it because, even if Sidney did offer to split with his Mrs, he'd be wasting his time as I was not prepared to have him as a brother-in-law.

Maybe I touched a nerve or something because she got a bit personal after that, and as I didn't want to get expelled from play school again I backed off. I suggested some People Watching which we did and I let her come second. Then we did the quiz in the *Echo* and I won because I'm very clever and she said it was a draw because she got that Botswana used to be Bechuanaland but that was because she read the answer upside down.

'So,' she said, 'let's go for the tie-breaker,' and I wondered what she was on about because there wasn't one. She pretended to read from the paper and said: 'Complete the following. People who have sidecars on their motor bikes are prats because . . .'

Very funny. She'd seen Malcolm come in. He stood there in the doorway looking like the one Bo-Peep gave up on. He waved. I winced. Then he came over and asked if we were ready for another which we weren't but this didn't stop Pam saying: 'Gin and orange please. Just a double 'cos I'm going soon.'

'Right,' he said, 'back in a mo',' and went.

She looked at me. I knew what she was thinking.

'Back in a mo'!' she said.

I felt defensive. OK, so he was a prat but he was buying the drinks. She shook her head and went on: 'I'm amazed you two have lasted. You and a birdwatcher. I mean it's a joke, isn't it?'

'There's nothing wrong with birdwatching,' I said. She put on her smirk face, so I continued.

'You don't know nothing, you, Pamela. It's a very interesting hobby. And it gets you out in the fresh air. It's time you realised that there's a lot more to life that three falls and a submission with Hissing Sid every second Wednesday.'

She de-smirked and came back with: 'Actually, if you're talking about open air pursuits Sidney and me often go for walks, in woods and things. He collects leaves.'

I was winning. On a Wally Scale of one-to-ten collecting leaves must be worth at least nine point five.

'And you scoff at me because old goofy over there is a birdwatcher,' I said.

'Goofy eh?' she said.

'It's all right for me to say it,' I reminded her (that's the rule).

'You're all talk,' she said. 'You've only been birdwatching once.'

Well, I couldn't let her get away with that.

'That's a lot you know,' I said. 'We're going Sunday.'

'Which Sunday?'

'This Sunday.'

'Since when?' she sneered.

'Planned it ages ago,' I said. 'We're going looking for the lesser-spotted gobtwit.'

'You've just made that up,' she said.

'I never,' I protested, and just then Malcolm appeared with the drinks. I thought we might have moved on to something else but our Pam has a touch of the bulldog in more than her features.

'Malcolm,' she said, 'what does the lesser-spotted gobtwit look like?'

'I've never . . .' he said but I stilettoed his instep and finished off for him.

'Never seen one, have you, Malc? They're very rare, aren't they. Which is why we're going looking for one on Sunday, aren't we.'

'Sunday?' he said.

'Yes, you know,' I said, without needing to *act* impatient. 'You and me are going birdwatching Sunday. Don't tell me you've forgotten.'

The penny dropped with a clang that must have woken them in Manchester. That's if anything can wake them in Manchester.

'Sunday, of course,' he said, and turned to Pam. 'We're going over to Flint. There's mudflats and the waders come in close. And there's woodlands near by. Conifers at the top end, but deciduous near the estuary. There's a good spot overlooking the bay between Mostyn Docks and the Point of Air, on the railway footbridge at Ffynongroew.'

Trust Malcolm; now that he'd got the idea he didn't know when to stop. I dozed as he blabbed and then I heard him say: 'With a bit of luck we might see one.'

'One what?' I said.

'Gobtwit,' he said.

'Lesser-spotted,' added Pamela, with disbelief written on every wrinkle.

Malcolm explained later that he'd gone on about the place in an effort to cover every type of habitat because at the time he didn't know what a lesser-spotted gobtwit was. I didn't tell him.

It was time to change the subject.

'What were we talking about?' I said.

'We were doing the competition,' Pamela said. 'Malcolm, why does your bike have a sidecar?'

'To stop it falling over,' I told her. 'Now just knock it off, Pamela.'

'No, I'm serious,' she said. 'Why does it?'

'It's for the hide,' he said. 'When I go birdwatching.'

Well, that confused her; and me, come to that, but I'd sense enough to keep my mouth shut. She just went in feet first.

'The hide?' she said. 'Do you mean when you've spotted it you kill the poor bugger and hang its skin in your sidecar?'

Malcolm then enjoyed a fit of the tee-hees like I'd

never seen before, and when he finally gurgled to a stop he explained that a hide is a sort of collapsible tent and that you sit in it to birdwatch. He then blabbed on with another five minutes' worth, but I didn't doze off this time; just sat there nodding and agreeing with him as if I'd known all the time, till finally when he'd finished I could say: 'See, Pamela, you're thick.'

She got sniffy and just said: 'And you're a liar,' as if that was news. Then she stood up and said: 'Anyway, I'm off to see another gobtwit. The greater spotted,' adding for my benefit, 'it's all right for me to say it.'

Malcolm asked what she'd meant by the last bit so I explained that it was to do with calling people names:

'Saying you're a long streak of frog's vomit is OK, provided it's me that says it.'

He seemed to understand because he gave his serious nod.

'Right, now about Sunday,' I said. 'When do we meet?'

'Ah now,' he said, 'I didn't like to actually say anything while Pam was actually here but, you know, we hadn't actually arranged anything.'

I actually counted to ten as an alternative to actually belting him, then explained gently: 'I know that, you daft pillock, but we've got to go through with it now, haven't we?'

'Yes,' he said. Then after a thought, 'Go through with what?'

I certainly pick 'em. I insisted he watched my lips while I spelt it out. 'Look, Malcolm,' I said, 'on Sunday we are going birdwatching, for reasons far too complicated for you to understand. Just get your wellies and your little canvas stool and pick me up at the flat late enough for Pamela to see us going. And bring the hide thingy. It'll be somewhere for me to go while you're out chasing the lesser-spotted gobtwit.'

'Got it,' he said.

'Good,' I told him. It had crossed my mind that we could just pretend to go but she'd be suspecting that

and with Malcolm as chief witness for the defence I'd
have had to spend so long rehearsing him it would be
easier to play for real and then maybe try some sort of
double bluff where you pretend to be caught out and
then let her cross-examine Malcolm.

'Got it,' he said again.

'OK,' I said. 'So you're a clever boy.'

'Limosa Lapponica,' he said. 'Limosa Lapponica, the
bar-tailed godwit. That's what you're thinking of.'

'No, Malcolm,' I said, 'but it'll do.'

CHAPTER FORTY

It had been the strangest interlude. At the time I
could only conclude that Brenda, during one of her
frequent visits to the library, must have been
browsing in Nat. Hist., Subsection Ornithology
(Dewey Number 598.2). With her penchant for mis-
pronunciation no doubt Godwit to Gobtwit was but a
short hop. Trouble was that if we were to see one that
weekend it would mean us making a much longer hop.
To Russia in fact (joke). They are, in fact, a very
rare breeder in this country. On the other hand if she
was prepared to wait a couple of months for the
autumn migration the Dee estuary would be teeming
with them.

Anyway, I was pleased to think that the outdoor
pursuit I had so recently postulated was actually to
happen. Some sixth sense perhaps? Maybe. And
maybe the slight unease mixed with confusion that
had accompanied our conversation in the pub was a
warning of the precipice beyond. Certainly there were
echoes of earlier meetings in the exchanges, and I
wasn't too sad when Pamela left. It seemed that,
whenever they blazed away, Muggins Malcolm got
caught in the crossfire.

Come Sunday am and I was loading the sidecar with accoutrements (birdwatching), as per list. I'm a great believer in lists. For instance I regularly draw up a, 'jobs for the weekend' list, as tasks can then be prioritised or grouped in the most efficient order. To illustrate with an actual occurrence, 'Checking the central heating header tank' and, 'Retrieving mother's weekend case' don't at first appear related. In fact, both involved a visit to the loft. Thanks to the list, I used the ladder only once.

Also there is considerable satisfaction in seeing that vertical column of ticks after an industrious weekend. Actually on one occasion, when I cleaned the grids early Saturday (emergency – excess of autumn leaves), I then wrote it on the list, and ticked it. Childish I know, but I felt it was earned.

So there I was, loading according to my standard birdwatching list. And top of the optional section (i.e. not always used) was 'Hide'. Then I remembered. I'd lent it to Leonard some time prior. Did it matter? Yes. Brenda had been most insistent. Panic. Ring Leonard. Have you ... ? Yes, sorry, should have returned; will bring round. No, not nec.; will pick up on way past.

They've a big detached, with a drive that sweeps up to the front door and back down to the road forty yards on. Dates from a time when not being able to turn the horses round was a problem. I make a point of always going in and out via the same gate. I suppose it's the Bolshevik in me.

We chatted briefly as I packed the hide into the sidecar. Leonard said he'd heard on *Birdline* that a Black-winged Pratincole had been seen out beyond Neston. Most unusual.

She was ready. Her clothes were a little more subdued than usual though her make-up could still have served as a TV Colour Test Card. I thought I might bring up the subject of camouflage some time – but not then.

She shouted loud goodbyes to Pamela interspersed with equally loud questions to me such as, 'Did you bring the hide?' and 'Have you got the millet?'

My answers didn't seem to matter.

As I headed back through the tunnel I got to thinking that Flint was a long way to go, especially as the godwits wouldn't be around until August. What's more we'd made a late start and from what she'd said it was as much the function of the hide that she was interested in. Next thing she was shouting in my ear about a café stop. More lost time. So that decided me. As we settled to our teas and one and a half ginger creams (why must they make them in packs of three?) I put it to her that Burton Marsh was nearer and there was a chance of seeing the Black-winged Pratincole, and was about to give more reasons when she said:

'OK. As long as you take the picture.'

She then took from her top pocket a camera that was about the size of a small tube of toothpaste; if you'd got it in a cracker you'd have been disappointed. I thought of my Minolta Dynax 7000i with the Sigma 28–200 super zoom attached and said: 'Don't worry, if we see the Prat, I'll use my own equipment.'

'What you prats do in the privacy of your own nest box is no business of mine,' she said. 'All I want is a picture of me with binoculars, hide and a large lump of outdoors in the background.' Essential evidence, she called it.

I then put it to her that if we were to go after the Pratincole there was no point in putting up the hide but she said she'd never seen a hide and was intrigued.

'Actually,' I said, 'they're meant for woodlands, and really should be put up for a few days before you intend to use them – so the birds get used to them.'

I then explained how the recognised procedure was for two people to go in together, and then one come out and walk away. She accused me of winding her up but I naturally denied. She still didn't believe and said:

'You mean birds can't count? They see two people go in, then one comes out so they think, "Hey, that tent must be empty. Let's go in out the rain." '

'They're very timid creatures,' I reminded her.

'Say if when the person comes out the bird doesn't see him,' she said. 'Maybe the bird has nipped along to the nest next door to borrow a cup of worms.'

Then she really got carried away.

'Or say if the bird sees you come out, but didn't see you go in. He'd think you had a tunnel to it.'

And on she rambled, ever onwards and upwards until I wondered if it wouldn't be better to call it quits and run her home there and then. Shades of our very first day out.

But when I suggested she wouldn't hear of it.

CHAPTER FORTY-ONE

I thought I was having one of them *déjà-vus*. You know, where you have the feeling that you've been there, done this, heard that, at some other time. Dead eerie they are, and all to do with this short circuiting in your left Cortès – or was he the Spanish bloke who killed millions of Aztecs because they weren't Christians and he was? That's the trouble with all this reading and watching Open University. You get mixed up.

Anyway, it wasn't. Turned out I had been there. Same caff, same bike, same Malcolm only he was Arnold then. The only thing new was when we stopped at a cross roads and he ceremoniously pointed to a big house with a brass plate on the gate.

'That's where Mrs Scott lives,' he said. 'Our vet.'

What can you say? Then on along the same old roads through boring Wirral, same dull hedges, same chunk of green nothing at the end. Everything just as we'd left it. They hadn't even had the council round to cut the dandelions. We parked by the same gate and trekked up this slope past a big rock that looked as if it was trying to escape from Cheshire – and could you blame it? We stopped near the hedge. Same hedge. All that was missing was a big black cloud in the distance quietly brewing up a Monsoon for the journey back.

'I'll put it up here,' he said.

He meant the hide.

'Or maybe over there, on the edge of the copse. On the other hand from here we can see down to the mud flats as well.'

He argued with himself for a bit longer until I made up his mind for him by taking the bag and emptying the lot over his feet.

'Might as well put it here,' he said.

He minced about with poles and guys and pegs like that white-faced Frenchman who's always putting up invisible deck chairs. I left him to it and climbed up the rock. I sat there for a bit but there was nothing to see but scenery so I came down.

'There it is,' he said, and there it definitely was.

It was like a short fat telephone box made from canvas the colour of week-old cow dung.

'You can't flake out in that,' I protested.

'Of course not,' he said. 'You sit on the stool and look out through here.'

He pointed to a flap with a bit of mesh behind it. There was a similar one on each side and half-way down the front a canvas tube stuck out. I guessed what it was for because he'd told me that they sometimes stay in a hide for hours and hours or even over night. But he said it was for a long lens camera.

'What now?'

'Well, we'll leave it for a bit,' he said. 'Go back to

140

the bike. Have some lunch. Then come back here and . . .'

But I stopped him there.

'Don't tell me everything at once,' I said. 'Too much excitement makes me go all sweaty.'

Lunch was very Malcolm with wholemeal cobs stuffed with shredded lettuce and carrot and other rabbit fodder. I wondered if it would give him ideas. My contribution was a large pack of ready salted and a bottle of Sidney's plonk which Pam had been saving in case we ever had a blocked sink. It tasted foul but we forced ourselves. That is until I noticed Malcolm was finishing each sentence with a giggle, so I took it off him.

He was prattling on about the hide and saying we weren't going to use it properly but it was all for my benefit so I asked if he wanted to use it improperly. And he giggled some more, burped, and then announced to all the watching wild life that we were ready to go.

When we got there he pulled back the flap and ushered me in. Two black eyes stared back. Seemed Sidney's plonk was even stronger than I'd thought. Then I realised that the eyes were attached to a sheep. We looked at each other for a bit the way you do – then I ushered him/her/it out. Him/her/it then gave Malcolm a smile of brotherly recognition before heading off for a gambol. Then we crawled in and I wondered what the watching birds would make of that. And that's when the fun really started, though not the sort of fun you nature lovers might expect. The first problem arose because we had each arrived in the hide with our own bum, but there was only one stool.

'You'll have to sit on my knee,' he said. It wasn't easy, and even when we'd settled I was still in pain, mainly because he seemed to be wearing his thigh bones outside his legs.

'It's going to be too hot,' he said. 'Should have taken our sweaters off.'

w.—8   141

Subtle, he ain't.

'I'll just loosen this,' he said.

I don't know what it was but he loosened it and a bit of me at the same time.

'Now I'll show you what to do,' he went on.

I thought, 'There's cheek,' but he meant with the binoculars.

'Look across towards the flats. Do you see anything?'

I looked; then told him that they must have the curtains drawn in the flats because it was just black. He said he meant the mud flats – then looked at the binoculars and said: 'Sorry, I've left the lens caps on.'

So he took them off and put them somewhere safe. Again I looked and that time everything was blurred, so he told me to twiddle the little thing in the middle but when I went to he nearly fell off the stool. But he was serious. So I twiddled the right bit and suddenly the blur turned to hundreds of birds all pecking away in the mud. He said they were mainly Sandpiper though one or two were not and I said I could tell that because they weren't the same colour but he said he meant K, N, O, T, and they were a bit early unless they were Dunlin but then they should have a black patch underneath. Then he wanted to really show off.

'Tell you what,' he said, 'you describe any bird you see and I'll tell you what it is.'

'Yes, Mr Attinbugger,' I said.

'You can look anywhere. Across to the trees if you like. I'll close my eyes.'

'No peeping,' I warned. 'Right. Brown speckled with orange legs.'

'Does it have a beak that turns up at the end?'

I agreed that it had and he preened and said: 'Redshank. Next.'

'Greeny black with a white belly and a flat head.'

'Sounds like a lapwing. Has it got feathers on its head?'

142

'Well, what do you expect, a balaclava?'

'Feathers that stick up?' he said.

'Definitely.'

'Then it's peewit.'

I told him to make up his mind but he said that a lapwing and a peewit were the same thing – so he definitely deserved it for being a clever clogs.

'Right,' I said. 'Speckled grey with blue stripes, long green legs and a red beak.'

He got quite excited.

'God knows,' he said, grabbing the binoculars. 'Here, let's have a look. Whereabouts was that one?'

'Nowhere,' I said. 'I've been making them up.'

Well, he got quite violent, but in a giggly sort of way, and I struggled in a wriggly sort of way and things might have progressed as they have been known to when two are gathered together in the hot dark for a wriggle and a giggle. But no. Not when one of the two is Stoneway M., Mackerel Extraordinary and Wally First Class.

Later he said that our combined weight plus wriggles made the rear legs of the stool sink into the ground so that he'd had to pull forward which strained his lumbar region which then locked so that he couldn't keep his balance anymore. But he would, wouldn't he. Truth was, he just fell over backwards, dragging me on top of him and causing the stupid hide to collapse on the pair of us.

If the birds were watching they'd have been in hysterics. Certainly B2 was having a smirk. Funny how she always turned up for any mackerel-made catastrophe. I decided one day to have a think about that.

Meanwhile, under the canvas, Malcolm was whining and groaning in my ear. I recognised the old, 'Don't shout at me for being a wally because I'm hurt' ploy.

'It's my back,' he moaned. 'It's stuck. I can't move.'

I told him not to be so stupid and to get up. B2 said she'd often thought we should have been a nurse. But he just lay there, so I struggled out and stood up. As I took a deep breath of the fresh air we'd come for, but hadn't had much of thanks to the sheep having left a deposit on the premises, I noticed two blokes coming up the slope. They waved. I didn't. In the distance I could see a sports car parked behind Malcolm's bike.

B2 was as puzzled as I was.

CHAPTER FORTY-TWO

It turned out that an intervertebral disc had prolapsed through the fibres of my spinal ligaments. Slipped is the common term, but somehow that devalues the pain.

It was fortunate that James and Leonard came along when they did. Otherwise I don't know how I'd have got home. They'd been in touch with *Birdline* and obtained the grid ref for the most recent siting of the Black Winged Pratincole. Not far from where we were as it turned out. Then they'd spotted the bike and were heading up the track to see if I'd had any luck. Just as well they didn't arrived five mins. sooner. Embarrassment plus plus.

Regarding the B.W.P. well, none of us got it. I subsequently apologised for spoiling things but they all said it didn't matter.

I was in no condition to introduce but they sorted themselves out. Brenda explained the situation and events leading to, and although her account was somewhat histrionic it carried the gist. They then improvised a stretcher from the hide and its support poles, and on the way down to the car only dropped me once.

With some difficulty they managed to lay me out in

the rear of Leonard's Morgan 4/4. Fortunately James is an experienced motor cyclist – he had a Triumph T140 for many years – so he was able to follow on my bike, as Leonard drove to Meols (with uncustomary restraint I'm grateful to add). Brenda sat up front and chatted away to Leonard in her usual jokey style – in order to keep my spirits up, I suppose.

It's good to have friends.

Once home I lay flat on the living room floor, as keeping the spine horizontal reduces the intervertebral pressure. There is an alternative to what might be termed the 'supine' school which recommends the 'hanging by the hands from the top of a convenient doorway' method as a form of natural traction but I had found this less effective in the early stages, besides being a minor impediment to others trafficking the premises. Mother rang the doctor ignoring Brenda's suggestion to contact Mrs Scott. Then she dusted round before getting out the vacuum cleaner.

It was a full hour and a half before he arrived and then it was a locum. He looked about twelve and, frankly, I knew more about my condition than he. Well, as you may have guessed, it had happened before – two and five-sixths years prior to be precise – and naturally I had read up on the subject. I've found that if you can use the correct terminology the medical profession are a touch less patronising. We agreed on rest as the first priority with pain killers as nec. Immediate manipulation is feasible in order to reduce intervertebral pressure and relax the ligaments sufficient to permit reduction of the protrusion. But I didn't tell him. Thought I'd just contact the osteopath who'd helped last time.

It was also decided that the centre of the living room floor was not an ideal convalescent area so with considerable difficulty I was helped to my room. My mother and Brenda then removed my outer garments each telling the other she could manage on her own. Their subliminal enmity resulted in a certain lack of co-operation with the process and the removal of my trousers was almost too painful to be embarrassing. I was glad when they left me to suffer in peace.

Slowly the pain killers took effect. As I drowsed I was vaguely aware of female voices droning below.

Then Brenda must have left. Perhaps she looked in and I was asleep.

Or perhaps not.

It was precipice time.

I guessed that her, 'Get Well Soon' card would be a rude one. You know the sort: 'Hurry up and get better. It's your round.'

But it wasn't, because she didn't send one. Nor did she call round, or ring. She'd told me once that she had just written fourteen pages to her cousin in Canada. I thought I was perhaps in line for a long letter – written over a few days – a week even. I gave it ten days, then in the evening I rang her. She was out, and Pam didn't know when she'd be back. Same next time. And when I rang in the afternoon there was no reply – except for once when an operator with a strange voice told me I'd mis-dialled. So I redialled and there was no reply.

I wrote twice. The first, short and to the point. The second, longer, mystified. Nothing. Maybe I should have tried to contact sooner – but I was bedridden – in pain – the phone was downstairs – writing is difficult from the horizontal.

And none of it made any sense. We hadn't rowed. Niggled, yes, but she was always niggling. Then I wondered if *she'd* been in an accident. A broken right hand perhaps. But Pam would have said. Pam had been very brief. I should have asked more.

So, what next? It was decision time. Should I do something and, if so, what? Or nothing? And, as a determinist, had I any choice? Well, yes, even to do nothing is to exercise a choice. Brenda always said that you had to make things happen but I didn't agree. I know things happen anyway. Then how come I'm talking about choice? Well, you see, 'to choose' is to select the desire which is strongest, and our desires are the product of our personality. And personality is fixed at birth. So even when we think we have made a choice that choice was inevitable given that we are who we are. So what did I choose? Well, I did decide to do *something* – what I couldn't decide was what to do.

So I waited another week, and although one pain lessened the other remained. I spent a lot of time remembering. Chester, the Motor Museum, Crewe Station. Sensibly these recollections should have emphasised how much better off I was without her, but somehow time had tinged them pink.

Then another week.

Back at work Terry was Terry. He told me the best cure was 'hair of the dog' and suggested a few kennels I might try. Then he went off for his fortnight's 'Eighteen to Thirty' in Malaga to help put back the cause of Anglo-Spanish relations another decade. He pitied my recently acquired ineligibility, though did say I might have passed for twenty-nine had I not looked so miserable. He was sure it would have been a great cure.

I was glad when he'd gone and I immediately reached a decision. I decided I would forget the whole affair, though it wasn't really an affair, but I'd forget it anyway. Well, I intended to, but it wasn't easy, and after a further week I decided to rescind the last decision.

I called at The Grapes a couple of times. At least I looked over the frosted part of the window, but there was nobody sitting by the space invaders. I didn't go round to the flat. No way could that have been a 'chance meeting': 'Hello, I'm collecting for Barnardo's. Good Heavens, do you still live here?'

I then reached another decision and decided that when Terry came back I'd take a week off myself. I couldn't really face the immediate post hol. tales of his Iberian Nights and by the time I got back his enthusiasm for detail might have waned a little.

The guest house in Norfolk was one I'd stayed at before. It's a favourite with Birders. I thought a lot, read a little, walked a lot, had a little (had a Little Bittern actually! – we birders say we 'had' a bird rather than we saw it. Thought I ought to make that clear). Had a day on Blakeney Point (conventional use of 'had'). It rained. Lots of Warblers about but missed out on a Great Snipe that called the day I left. Walked into the village. Sent her a card.

It was a goodbye card, with a PS. I'd thought it through. Decided to make it my last shot so to speak. If she didn't respond then amen. The Brenda Chronicle could be confined to the pedal bin of history.

I was home by midday on the Saturday. My mother immediately started with assorted back numbers of the week's inconsequentials. After two hours I escaped to the garage for a tinker and a mooch. I decided that although it was all over I would, as part of the final interment, make one last call at The Grapes. If she was there I'd go in, sort out, get explanation; then, loose ends tied – end of story. If she wasn't there, then end of story anyway. New life Sunday et seq.

I took the train. As often happens, what seemed black and white turned out to have a grey possibility. I peeped. She wasn't there, but Pam was, with Sidney. Decision time.

I decided to go in, but only half-heartedly.

As I crossed to the bar I glanced across and played surprised to see them. They acknowledged so I altered course.

'Long time no see,' said Sidney, a past master of the *cliché juste*. I asked if I could get them a drink. Pamela accepted but Sidney was moving on. It was his wife's birthday and he'd bought her a single yellow rose. Romantic, but cheap. He left.

148

I'm not a drinking person but on this occasion the bitter went down far too easily. Conversation was initially somewhat stilted. Her job was much the same. Sidney was OK. My back was better. My holiday was good. Yes, the card had arrived. Brenda? Brenda was OK. Out a lot. Yes, a lot.

Pamela bought a round.

Tentatively I enquired further. Going with anyone? There'd been a few – she thought. I played with a beer mat. With half of it overlapping the table I could flick it up with the back of my fingers and catch it in one movement. A modest skill but mine own.

For the next round Pamela switched to straight orange so I supplemented my third pint with crisps. Harold was at his myopic usual and supplied cheese and onion although I distinctly asked for roast ox. Must admit I didn't notice until they were half gone. We, I, was talking about our first meeting, and how Brenda had made out that Pamela was a lady wrestler. Pamela remembered.

She drained her glass and I asked if she wanted another but she said she didn't and that I should go easy. I explained that I'd come in on the train and I showed her my ticket. Then I ate a crisp and talked some. Then I ate another crisp except that due to an element of dextral confusion it was my ticket. We laughed.

I reminisced some more. Then Pamela said she'd have to go but I suggested another and she said definitely no. But I was feeling masterful and told her to sit there while I went for them, and I stood up and she stood up but she seemed to sway a bit and I grabbed her and she fell backwards onto the bench with me on top of her.

Which must have been just as the door opened.

CHAPTER FORTY-THREE

The postcard had a picture of some wellied wally peering over a hedge with binoculars the size of a couple of two litre Coke bottles. It was titled 'Twitching in Norfolk'. On the other side was our address including post-code – which was more than I knew, and the message in joined-up writing:

'Goodbye Brenda,

Yours sincerely,

Malcolm.

PS. I'll be home Saturday.'

Pathetic, but then he always had been. I thought back to that day in the hide. I remembered his plaintive moans from the back of the car as we drove over Thurstaston Hill although we were going at hearse pace. Usually it's a real 'hold on to your hair piece' sort of trip with Len. Then I thought of him lying on the living room floor like a beached porpoise while his mother vacuumed round him. Then getting him up to bed and trading black looks with her as we got his trousers off. And who else would have boxer shorts with 'Save the Panda' on them? Pathetic.

Len, of course, was a very different barrel of worms. Good for a good time, but not one to take your eye off. He liked to play Mr Yuppie which is OK by me – it's a free country if someone else is buying. But then there were a couple of times when I got the odd vibe that I was being shown off as the pet Scouse scally.

James was nicer, but still inclined to the occasional 'Absolutely' which I suppose is better than, 'OK, yah'. Trouble with him was that I got the feeling there'd been something a bit heavy around in the not too distant. Still, we had some fun. The trip to Anglesey was good and against my better judgement I even got to enjoy a bit of birdwatching – but there was time to grow out of it.

You might think all this a bit mean on the mackerel but don't blame me, it was her idea. After he'd been de-bagged and tucked up she'd suggested a cup of something before I went. I didn't know she meant pesticide. As we supped she started in with the 'girls together', 'heart to heart', 'everybody's best interest' bit. Now maybe when the hide collapsed I'd caught a thump on the head but it's for sure I wasn't operating too quickly in that area. She was a good five minutes into the sisterly chat before I realised I was being warned off. Not the red card. Far more subtle. Just the reminder of how little we had in common. He had responsibilities. I didn't. There would always be problems. He couldn't change and I wouldn't want to. Clever, that.

An earlier Brenda would have told her where to go and how to use the Paxo when she got there. But the earlier Brenda would never have found herself stuck in that Meols mausoleum in the first place. She would never have put up with him for so long. And that was the problem. I mean, as far as I was concerned it was no big deal. Never had been. He was no catch, and to argue made it seem he was. Well, I did a bit, but just because I didn't like the idea of her telling me what to do. Then she came with the old compromise suggestion.

People do it, don't they. Find a problem that isn't there, then solve it with a line that suits nobody and make out that they are the only one being reasonable. 'Why not just not see each other for a bit? See how you both feel afterwards. Have a look round. You are still very young. Can't beat variety. Why, when I was a girl . . .' (When she was a girl they chased you with clubs.) 'Think what you're missing. This is the ideal time with him laid up for a while.'

I asked, sarky like, what Malcolm thought of all this. She said they'd had a chat only the other day and he had agreed that we didn't have much in common. In fact he'd listed the things he liked that I didn't. He'd even said I was like her in that respect.

Now, there are insults, and there are insults, and I've been known to let the odd one slip out myself, on rare occasions, but never anything like that. *Me,* like *his*

151

mother! And he must have said it! She wouldn't have dared make up something like that in case I checked. Fortunately for the sake of the mausoleum and its inhabitants on both floors the door bell rang at that moment.

It was Leonard. He'd found Malcolm's binoculars in the back of the car. How was Malcolm? Asleep, poor lamb. So it *was* his brother in the hide. Leonard said cheerio and as I'd just about got my voice back I was able to ask if he was going past the station. He was.

In fact we went a lot further.

B2 was very wary but I told her I could handle it. And I did, and Len was a lot of fun, and B2 huffed off. But not for long. A few days later she whinges back in saying it was a bit tight the way we'd dumped the Mackerel. I didn't think so. No way, but that night in bed I agreed to play pros and cons till finally I won and we agreed he was definitely one for the history shelf. That settled, we still couldn't sleep. I accused B2 of keeping me awake and told her I had noticed that she only seemed to come round after Mackerel-inspired disasters. She said that that was just my imagination and I said that so was she, so she said that if that was the case and he was now history then she could retire, and I said good. But she didn't. She waited till I was dozing and then got me thinking about him again:

We couldn't have been more different. Suppose his old girl was right on that score. He had two speeds, dead slow and stop; I get bored waiting for my toast to pop up. He's always, well at least when I let him, rambling on about life being all mapped out and how when you think you've a choice you haven't really, whereas if I thought this was all there was, and that you couldn't change things, I'd stick my head in at Gas Mark Seven. Then why did it last?

Curiosity, B2 reckoned. First of all, when we met him, we didn't believe it. When we had to believe it, we wondered how it ticked. And when we saw how it ticked, we didn't believe it again.

Similarities? None really. Well, perhaps one. He was a bit of a loner – and coped. He had to. And I am, but from choice. Like I say, I bore easily, and that includes with people. I suppose it was interesting seeing how he managed, but that was all.

Now Leonard couldn't have been more different – from him. Which isn't to say he was like me, though he did like things fast, and we did get in a lot of living in a pretty short time. It was great when we were on our own and we got about a fair bit. But it got sour back in his plastic local where he liked to play centre stage for a gang of mixed dung flies. It was there that I caught the odd word, the quick glance that signalled that I was being laughed at and not with. From that moment his days were numbered. I just had to make sure that the toffee set knew who dropped who and who for.

The three weeks with James were pretty good too but again I needed to move smartish when I first got the sense of not so keen. Maybe the previous heavy was back in circulation; anyway I called it quits – before he did.

Then came the postcard.

I looked at it again as the train pulled into Meols station. Fancy putting 'Yours sincerely' on a postcard.

He was out. No, she didn't know where. Yes, I had kept my side of the bargain but six weeks wasn't very long. Six months would have been better. Would she not have preferred six years, or sixty even? There was no need to be sarcastic.

I left.

Pamela had said she'd be in early but there was no sign. I guessed The Grapes.

I must admit that it came as something of a shock to walk in on the spectacle of one horizontal Stoneway attempting to have his evil way with my sister. Around that time B2 had been going on a bit about my behaviour, but there'd been nothing like that. Then we remembered who the participating parties were, and we waited for the reasonable explanation.

153

We were not impressed. They claimed he had fallen on her after consuming three pints of Harold's bitter. Hardly enough to produce a hiccup. Still, I was ready to be gullible. Pam said she'd nip home and put the black coffee on simmer. Leave us to chat.

We didn't for a bit. Then he said: 'I've eaten my ticket.'

Quite a conversation stopper, except that we hadn't even started. I asked him how Norfolk was and he said it was flat and laughed a lot; then said it wasn't an original joke because he'd heard it in a play that the Chrysanthemums did and I said it wasn't even a joke and wondered why I'd just been to Meols.

Then B2 nudged me to go easy and I was piqued and told her she could take over, and I watched.

They talked, carefully, piecing together the six weeks. He didn't know about his mother's suggestion, but he had said the things she said he'd said, but not meant them the way she said he meant them. Then B2 fed feely questions and his answers showed that he didn't know we'd been a bit more than friendly with his two less than friends. We decided we'd tell him – sometime – not then.

He couldn't understand why letters hadn't arrived and B2 lied, 'What letters?' but he didn't believe. And they talked some more about old times and every now and then he showed that he was a natural athlete by flicking and catching a beer mat. Then he said how lucky it was that Len and James had happened by that time and B2 said a sarky 'Not 'arf,' so I pushed her under the seat before she said any more.

Of course I still didn't fancy him. Not like having the hots for someone – like they do in books – or you did yourself over pop stars when you were ten. But I was sort of comfortable again. Relaxed. And there weren't many people I felt like that with. Not many blokes anyway. Well, none – at the time. I suppose it was because he was nice – a yukky word, but it fits. And niceness sort of rubs off, and you feel that other people who yesterday were prats maybe aren't quite so bad and you should make allowances, and maybe they've got a sick budgie at home, and you feel a bit better and a bit warmer and if I don't stop this I'll vomit.

He flicked the beer mat.

'So,' he said, 'where do we go from here?'

'Ours for coffee,' I said, but he said he was thinking on the larger scale so I said that at most I only ever thought of the next seven days and: 'Let's see what we make of that.'

He thought for a bit.

'A week,' he said.

With answers like that plus his beer mat skills next stop had to be the Krypton Factor.

'Well,' he said, 'there is Friday. Are you doing anything?'

I thought for a bit as if I might have been, before saying I wasn't.

'Good,' he said. 'It's just that my mother will be going on the Tuesday with Alice Connolly because her husband lacerated his shin with a grass strimmer and it got infected and he has to rest it and she doesn't particularly want to go twice and she had suggested I might want to take a friend but I haven't seen Leonard for ages. So we've got four tickets and you'd like Peggy because I've told her about you and they're not at all like sisters and Bernard's always good for a laugh. OK then?'

'Tickets for what?' I dared ask.

'*Iolanthe*,' he said.

And it was as if I'd gone round in this great big loop and got absolutely nowhere.

'Me?' I said. '*Io*-bloody-*lanthe*? You've got to be joking.'

'Oh,' he said. And his lip quivered and he flipped his beer mat. But I couldn't, could I? Say if one of my mates found out.

Then he reminded me that I'd once said that you should always be ready to try things, and I said that as a general rule that was true but there were exceptions, like crack, and lion-taming, and *Iolanthe*. And he said: 'Oh.'

So it was my turn. I took a deep breath.

'What about tomorrow?' I said. 'Birdwatching?'

He was surprised. Well, I had done a bit. Shut up, B2.

'OK,' he said, and flipped and grinned. 'We could go looking for the lesser-spotted gobtwit.'

'I think I've found it,' I said.

And then he sort of leant across and sort of kissed me and it was all right. And I looked over his shoulder and there was Cedric and some of the others doing synchronised grinning, and I was going to signal them a score of *deux pointes*. But didn't.

He was OK, was Malcolm, and with practice might learn to kiss. And what did it matter what people thought? I could just lay back and think of Birdland.

'Malcolm,' I said softly, 'do that again.'

And he smiled that lopsided smile of his and said: 'OK.'

And flipped the beer mat.

THE END

THE BOY WHO SHOT DOWN AN AIRSHIP
by Michael Green

In this first part of his autobiography, Michael Green, author of the bestselling *Art of Coarse* books, treats us to an account of growing up in the 1930s and 1940s that is both hilarious and moving. Indeed, it was his adventures as a Leicester schoolboy, as an ill-fated cub reporter and as an accident-prone young soldier learning the facts of life, that inspired the comic series that would later become a household word.

The Boy Who Shot Down an Airship is at times comic, at times nostalgic, the picture of a thirties childhood vividly remembered and the frankest, funniest portrait for years of life in khaki.

'Good "coarse", high-spirited stuff'
Punch

'The Boy Who Shot Down an Airship is funny and nimbly written, but it's the small details of a vanished England that give the book its special flavour'
Evening Standard

'A lovely read ... these poignant, funny memoirs are his best work. *Treat yourself*'
Sunday Times

0 553 17607 2

THE CAT WHO CAME FOR CHRISTMAS
by Cleveland Amory

Cleveland Amory was an unsentimental, middle-aged journalist and author who preferred dogs. But one white Christmas Eve, not so long ago, he found himself in a deserted New York alley trying to rescue a starving, hurt, and not-at-all friendly cat.

Thus began the odd-couple relationship between a bachelor writer and a stray cat with a mind of his own which resulted in this extraordinary bestseller.

If you have ever owned a cat yourself or, as they say, been owned by one, you will recognize and delight in the seesaw odyssey which followed that Christmas Eve encounter. Just the chapter headings will tell you, as in 'His First Trip', 'His Fitness Programme', 'His Hollywood', 'His Domestic Policy', that where Polar Bear was stubborn, and Cleveland Amory determined, they compromised . . . and did it the cat's way.

0 553 17523 8

LOVE AND MARRIAGE
by Bill Cosby

The hugely successful author of FATHERHOOD and
TIME FLIES is back – funnier and truer than ever!

Tender but racy, naughty but very, very nice. Cosby
is back – bringing love and marriage together again
in the way only Cosby can.

0 385 26896 3